Blue Di

by

Dan Vandenberg

PublishNation
www.publishnation.co.uk

Chapter I

London, Friday, 17th June 1983

Sophie was perched on the edge of the bed, running her fingers along her sheer stockings – not only to check for flaws, but also because it felt so damn good. She stood up and walked over to her full length dressing mirror. Slim and leggy, she had a body honed by more than twenty years of serious swimming. *Not bad for thirty-four*, she thought, swinging her hips like a showgirl. *Not bad at all.*

It was nearly 6.00pm – time to slip into her Little Black Dress. She was going to a media party at a duplex apartment in Knightsbridge. Her boss was Sandy Johnson, founder and director of SJ Associates, a London advertising agency. In 1979, before he retired as a full colonel, their paths had crossed during a major exercise in Canada. At the time she was serving in the Women's Royal Army Corps as an analyst (special intelligence) with the rank of second lieutenant. His first impression had been a lasting one, and two years later he was more than happy to take her on as an account executive. She was on top of the job in nothing flat.

Sophie was barely four years old when her mother, Elizabeth, died in 1953 at the tragically early age of 26. Her father, Dominik Zoborski, had met Elizabeth in Liverpool, having arrived in October 1945 by ship from Poland. He was a quiet, thoughtful, very private man who had had to adapt to the demands of being a single-parent. When Sophie started to shine as a swimmer, he had socialised within a small group of acquaintances at the local swimming club; he never remarried. As Sophie grew into adulthood, she became a bittersweet reminder of what he had lost.

She was beyond pretty, and consequently had become accustomed to the kind of men who couldn't – or wouldn't – see beyond her looks. What relationships she had tended to be short and sporadic. Her bright, easy-going personality hid a deeply introspective alter ego.

Sophie had hardly seen Giles, a captain in the Royal Army Ordnance Corps, since taking up her new job. Despite the fact that he'd helped with the move to her basement flat in Bermondsey, she had already decided it was time for him to go. *I'll call him at the weekend*, she thought, *and break it to him gently*.

She had never really been in love with him. He thought he loved her, but in reality it was the sex with her that he loved – and there is a difference. She had found it increasingly difficult to tolerate his selfishness and general lack of interest in anything that wasn't painted green.

It was June 1983, and Britain – still enjoying the feel good factor of a remarkable victory over Argentina in the Falklands conflict – was pulling herself out of recession. The Bank of England had reduced the base rate to 9.56 per cent, and more and more people were opting to buy their own homes, apparently undeterred by mortgage interest rates of around 13 per cent. Johnson was determined to ride this wave of optimism, and had recently landed another prestigious account. It meant launching a new family hatchback, just the sort of big budget campaign he had always wanted. He mentioned the new campaign to Sophie in the taxi on the way to Knightsbridge – and he also had some other news.

'By the way, I've decided to give you a company car.'

'Are you sure I really need one in London?'

'We do have clients somewhat further afield, you know. It's a Saab 99 GL. I thought you'd be pleased…'

'I am... it's just that I've still got Gerald.'

'Gerald?'

'My VW Fastback.'

'Stick to the Saab when you're on company business – okay?'

'You're so masterful, Sandy. I'm not parting with Gerald, though. He means too much to me.'

'Masterful? Since when? If I'm not careful those high heels of yours will walk all over me. Incidentally, I think your VW might be a future classic. They weren't exactly a common sight on the roads when they were new.'

When they walked in to the party, 'Cantaloupe Island' by Herbie Hancock was playing in the background. She could stand a little jazz. After working the room for about twenty minutes, they were spotted by Johnson's star director, Tony Arnold. He'd produced a string of

2

award-winning TV commercials, and now Hollywood was beckoning. When he came over she went for a straightforward handshake. He took her hand, but then grabbed her waist before kissing her somewhat lingeringly on both cheeks. 'Where have you been hiding this one?'

'Not really hiding,' said Johnson. 'Sophie's been working overseas for a while. She'll be taking the lead on this new account – the car commercial.'

'I'm sure we'll make a great team,' said Arnold.

She smiled – but only to be polite. He was in his early forties, but clearly wanted to look younger. His gleaming white teeth were too neat, too perfect, to be totally natural. His beige suit was from Rodeo Drive. It was cut cleverly to disguise his lack of height and spare tyre; his hair was tied back in a ponytail, and he had a moustache and goatee. And he was more than a little hyper. She reckoned he'd been indulging in something more than just the champagne and canapés.

'What sort of budget are we looking at, baby?'

She had taken an instant dislike to him – and not just because he called her 'baby'. Knowing how important the campaign was, she didn't let it show. 'About two hundred thousand... I'll send you the schedule when we get the green light.'

'Tony's just bought a new BMW,' said Johnson.

'This is my second, a 635CSi – I love the look of it, and it goes like stink. I used to have an Aston Martin DB5, but mechanically it was just too labour intensive. I doubled my money when I sold it, so I wasn't that sorry to see it go.'

Arnold reached inside his jacket. He opened a fresh pack of cigarettes and offered one to Sophie, king size with a filter tip. She declined. 'Not your brand?'

'I don't smoke.'

Not for the first time his eyes checked her out like he was making a photocopy. 'A body like yours doesn't just happen. How do you keep in shape?'

'I swim.'

He grinned, then took a long, deep drag, exhaling the smoke through his nose and mouth. It curled around his face for a few

3

moments before being scooped up by the air-conditioning. 'I've got a heated pool. Feel free to come over whenever you like.'

She was non-committal: 'So are you a keen swimmer?'

'Not really, baby. I don't need to be – I'm naturally fit.'

Of course you are, you creep... how stupid of me.

'We need to talk about this new campaign,' said Johnson.

'There's a new Italian in the village,' suggested Arnold. 'We can meet at my place and then eat there.'

'What's wrong with a working lunch in the office?' Sophie was making mischief, and her comment did not go down too well with Arnold – his face fell like an avalanche, right down to his brown suede shoes.

'Italian sounds fine,' said Johnson, quickly.

'Isn't it time we made a move?' she said, raising her eyebrows expectantly.

As Sophie said her goodbyes and headed for the door, Arnold spoke quietly into Johnson's ear: 'You must bring that chick along with you. I definitely want to see more of her.'

'She'll be with me, never fear. Twelve-fifteen alright?'

'I can't wait.'

When they were outside, she flipped open her compact and checked her make-up. 'Thinking of going on somewhere?' asked Johnson.

'It's getting late, and I'm ready for bed.'

'Debbie's picking me up... she should be here any minute now.'

'I'll go and find a cab.'

'Don't be silly – we'll drop you off.'

'But my place is miles out of your way.'

'It's not that far... here she is.'

A mink metallic Jaguar XJ6 cosied-up to the kerb. He opened the nearside passenger door and Sophie glided on to the back seat. 'You don't mind taking this young lady home, do you darling?'

'Of course not – it's good to see you again, Sophie.'

'It's still very kind of you.'

'Don't mention it. I love driving this when Sandy needs a taxi service – he doesn't like my little Honda.'

4

'It's not that I dislike it, darling – I simply prefer a more comfortable conveyance.'

'Sandy's giving me a company car.'

'And so he should. I hope it's something decent.'

'I think Sophie will find a Saab decent enough.'

'You'll enjoy driving that. How did the party go?'

'Quite well, I think.'

'Sophie's far too modest – she was a big hit with everyone.'

'Was Tony there?'

'Oh yes,' said Sophie.

'You know, I haven't quite forgiven Sandy for inviting him to our garden party last year. I was rather glad to see him go, I must say.'

'I could hardly have *not* invited him, darling.'

'Those clammy hands of his,' said Sophie, 'and I *hate* cigarette smoke.'

'I accept,' said Johnson, 'that he's not exactly everyone's cup of tea... but just wait till you see him working. No one can fill a frame like Tony. And he knows exactly how to light everything. He's the best in the business.'

'As long as he concentrates on that side of things, we'll get along just fine.'

'Didn't he lose his father when he was very young?' said Debbie.

'I'm afraid so – he was beaten up so badly by the Stern Gang that he died in hospital. It happened towards the end of the British Mandate in Palestine. Tony was only eight at the time. Apparently his poor mother had a complete breakdown – that's why he was put into care. It can't have been easy for him.'

'That's no excuse,' said Sophie. 'Anyway, I'm glad we left when we did... these heels are killing me.'

'I'll never understand why you wear those things.'

'Flat shoes would hardly have matched my dress now, would they? Or my drop earrings and pendant.'

'They really suit you,' said Debbie. 'Amethysts, aren't they?'

'Giles bought them for my birthday. It was sweet of him... he's bought me some nice things, I must say.'

'Could he be the one, do you think?'

5

'No – we've been drifting apart for ages. I'm going to tell him it's over. Please don't let Tony know that, Sandy. The last thing I need is for him to think I'm unattached.'

'Don't worry, you can count on my discretion. That said, you're not getting any younger…'

'Neither is anyone else… it's called the ageing process.'

He stifled a yawn. 'I suppose you're right. Debbie and I have been lucky. It was love at first sight, wasn't it, dearest?'

'If you say so. I have to admit you did look rather dashing in your dress uniform.'

The time had passed quickly, and they nearly overshot her flat. 'Anywhere here is fine,' she said.

'You must come over for dinner again,' said Debbie.

'You can stay over if you like,' said Johnson.

'I'd like that very much. Thanks again for the lift. Take care.'

She kicked off her heels the moment she was inside. Bliss! Then she took a shower and went straight to bed, making a mental note to call Giles in the morning.

Saturday. 18th June, 7.00am

Sophie tended to rise early – even on weekends. It was a routine ingrained even before she joined the army. From the age of 12 she'd been in the local swimming pool by seven most mornings, training like a demon. She treated herself to a red grapefruit for breakfast, together with a mug or two of tea and a bowl of cornflakes. Her radio was usually tuned to BBC Radio 4, a habit she'd picked up in the army. She liked to feed both mind and body.

She checked the time. Her Omega De Ville was another present from Giles. It was a little after nine. Apart from the pendant it was quite the best thing he had ever given her. But she could not be bought at any price, and this was no time for sentimentality: his time was up. By now he would be back from breakfast in the officers' mess: 'Hello… is that you Giles?

'You've taken your time, haven't you?'

'Sorry… I've just been incredibly busy…'

'Do you know how long it's been? Three weeks at least.'

'I've said I'm sorry.'

'Well, as it happens, something's come up.'

6

'Oh...?'

'I've got an exchange posting in the States.'

That's good, she thought. *Go and bore those nice Americans for a change.*

'Are you still there, Sophie?'

Of course I'm still here. 'Where are they sending you?'

'Aberdeen Proving Grounds.'

She couldn't quite believe it. 'That's great news, Giles. You've worked hard for that. You deserve it.'

'Thanks... there was a lot of competition for it. To be honest I didn't think I'd get it.'

'It's probably come at the right time. We hardly spoke the last time we met.'

'We're talking now, aren't we?'

'Only because we have to. It's pretty clear we're moving in different directions – literally.'

'That doesn't mean – '

'I think I made a mistake – and that's not so much your fault as mine. I'd rather be honest with you than come up with some pathetic excuse.'

'I know what your problem is – you've got some kind of father complex. That's why you're casting me aside, just like all the others.'

'Spare me the amateur psychology, Giles. I was hoping we'd be able to part on good terms.'

'Well, clearly we're not.'

The next thing she heard was silence. 'Hang up on me, then,' she said out loud. After cradling the receiver for a few seconds, she dropped it from just above the cradle. All things considered, he'd gone fairly quietly. There would be no last weekend, no final fling...

She topped up her mug of tea and began to reflect on their on their ten-month relationship. Old Beery Breath had had his moments, but he was never going to be her soulmate; he was too selfish, too shallow. After washing up, she put her clothes out on the bed. Blue jeans, army tee shirt, denim jacket. Her swimsuit, towel and shampoo were already packed.

South Bermondsey railway station was only just around the corner. She hopped on a train to Crystal Palace and then walked the short distance to the stadium. The 50 metre Olympic pool hadn't changed from when she last swam there for the army. And the changing rooms were just as basic. But it was good to get back in the water – she hadn't been in a pool for nearly a fortnight. There was no point in going for a time – too many swimmers were in the way. After a few lengths, she gained the distinct impression that someone was pacing her. He was an athletic, dark haired man with a light tan and Bermuda shorts.

For the next 50 metres she decided to see what Mr Bermuda Shorts could do. She tumble-turned and kicked, then poured on the power. Fellow swimmers gave her the room, and she stayed comfortably ahead, touching the wall with a good ten metres to spare. She stopped to see if her shadow would stop, or turn and carry on. He stopped alright. He was so out of breath that, for half a minute, he could hardly speak.

He was ruggedly handsome, Mediterranean-looking with broad shoulders and brown eyes. She liked brown eyes. He was older than her; late thirties, she thought. He had a scar, almost certainly from a bullet wound, just below his right collar bone. At last he could manage a sentence: 'You're quick... too quick for me!'

'I was holding back. I didn't want to embarrass you.'

He flashed a smile. 'Mind if I ask you a question?'

'As long as you don't mind the answer.'

'Where do you hide the propeller?'

She laughed. 'No propeller, just all those hours of training going back to my teens.'

They shook hands. 'I'm Sam, pleased to meet you.'

'Sophie, likewise.'

'I saw you at the party.'

'Last night?'

'For sure. I tried to say hello but you were preoccupied.'

'Yes – sorry about that. Do you know Tony Arnold?'

'Only by reputation. Friend of yours?'

8

'Hardly. I was introduced to him by my boss, Sandy Johnson. Apparently he's the greatest when it comes to directing commercials – he certainly seems to think so. Do you work for an agency, Sam?'

'Not exactly. Where can we talk?'

'I've nothing planned...'

'Not today. I have to be somewhere else.'

'Someone waiting for you?'

'I have to work.'

'On a Saturday?'

'Kind of goes with the job.'

Then he was out of the water and gone.

She did another 800 metres – but not for the exercise. Meanwhile, 'Sam', real name Samuel Segev, was picked up in a silver VW Golf. The driver was Abel Berkowitz, head of station for the Mossad. He was a short, barrel-chested, bull of a man who, like Segev, was ex-special forces. 'So, what can you tell me?'

'She's a cool one, for sure.'

'Then we need to apply a little pressure, don't we?'

'There's a limit to what we can do over here.'

'Don't go soft on me, my friend. We know she's going to see Arnold on Monday. We know what he's like with women. Let's give her a reason to hate him. We'll arrange a little accident, something to keep her boss out of the way.'

'She already dislikes him – it wouldn't take much.'

'We'll soon find out how cool she really is...'

Sophie went straight back to the flat and had lunch – tinned ravioli with grated cheese. 'I haven't much in,' she said to herself, 'and I need to take my dress to the dry cleaners.' So she went shopping. When she came back her LBD was still draped over the armchair. She wasn't usually so forgetful...

The sound of the traffic murmuring in the background was peaceful but uninspiring. So she delved into her record collection, quickly finding one of her favourite albums: 'Tapestry', by Carole King. She loved the upbeat tempo of 'I Feel the Earth Move'.

She washed down the omelette she had for supper with two glasses of pinot grigio. After sleeping in a little on Sunday morning, she decided it was time for some modest home improvements. Up

9

went some new curtains and lamp shades. And the cushions on the settee and armchair were given a complete makeover. Then she turned her attention to the bathroom, leaving it with a showroom shine. What she couldn't do was wipe Segev out of her mind – mainly because she didn't want to.

Monday, 20th June

Sophie was behind her desk at just after eight, having avoided the worst of the overcrowding on the Underground. Johnson always drove his Jaguar to the office. Just after nine, his PA, Georgie Trevino, was chatting to Sophie when she took a call from his car phone. 'Tell Sophie she'll have to fly solo. I'm afraid someone's run into the back of Debbie's car and then driven off. She's alright, just a bit shaken. I'm just heading back to help with the aftermath.'

A blonde Essex girl in her early twenties, Georgie was a superb organiser – as well as being eye candy for clients. She gave Sophie the message, then handed her the folder containing the outline for the new campaign. They both laughed at the tag line: 'The Car That's Full of Surprises'.

'If you ask me,' said Georgie, 'the biggest surprise is that they built the thing in the first place. It's hideous!'

'It's not going to sell itself, that's for sure. Still, that's what we pay our star director for, isn't it?'

'Watch yourself with him, Sophie. He's tried it on with me a few times...'

'I'll be careful... and I can always escape in my new Saab.'

'That's true. It's parked in one of our designated spaces... the attendant's got the keys. Sandy's kept a spare set – just in case.'

It was only a short walk to the underground car park off Berkeley Square. The Saab had at least one surprise, which the attendant demonstrated. To start, the car had to be in reverse gear (with the clutch depressed). And, after switching off, the key could not be withdrawn unless reverse was selected. After all those years of thrumming along in her Fastback, the refinement and performance of the 99 was certainly impressive. By 11.00am she was on the A3 approaching Guildford, a place she knew only too well from her initial training with the Corps.

She'd been looking in the rear view mirror more frequently than usual – and not just to check her make-up. She took the turn off for Farnham, and then headed down the leafy lanes to her destination, the charming little village of Kingly Brook.

Tony Arnold's house was classic mock Tudor with a twist – the twist being a double garage tacked on the side without any apparent regard for aesthetics. His Mercedes G-wagen and 635CSi were parked outside, and he was removing a slim aluminium case from the latter as she drew up alongside.

'Good morning, Tony.'

'Just you?'

'Debbie's had a bump.'

'Well, that's a damn shame, isn't it?' His insincerity was blinding. 'You know what they say? Two's company...'

She had expected him to hit on her. And she was going to humour him – up to a point.

'That trouser suit does look good on you.' He was photocopying again, this time more overtly.

He was dressed for something other than a business lunch: baggy black tee shirt, black jeans and trainers. 'Would you like to see my new toy?'

He picked up an aluminium case and she followed him under a stone arch overgrown with ivy. Beyond it was a rose garden flanked by a perfectly manicured lawn. They passed a row of erotic figures clearly inspired by the Kama Sutra.

'Brought them back from India last year,' he said, answering a question she hadn't felt the need to ask. 'Look at the way they're carved... so intricate, so tactile.'

She could also see tennis courts, and a swimming pool of dazzling blue.'We can go for a swim if you like.'

'I didn't bring anything...'

'That doesn't matter, it's heated... and we're not overlooked by anyone.'

'Some other time, perhaps.'

He flipped open the case and began to assemble a .22 Walther Olympia target pistol. 'I've been looking for one of these for ages.

This one's dated Nineteen Thirty-Six, though the seller didn't know if was used in the Games or not.'

'German quality. They've certainly stood the test of time.'

'Know about guns, do you?'

'I learned a lot of things in the army.'

'I find shooting very therapeutic. It helps to clear my mind.'

That shouldn't take very long.

He was balancing the pistol in his hand, getting the feel of it. 'I've got quite a collection actually, all in working order. I enjoy stripping and cleaning them.' He was about to load the Walther, but then had second thoughts. 'I'll try it later. Let's go inside.'

He lit a cigarette as they walked along the patio into the living room. 'You don't mind if I smoke?'

'It's your house.'

'Not for much longer. I'm moving to Malaga.'

Things are looking up.

'The removal vans start arriving later this week. I'm shipping everything out from Portsmouth on the ferry.'

'I expect Sandy knows about this?'

'Didn't he tell you? He's all for it, actually. It saves travelling backwards and forwards all the time. I've got a villa over there. Spain's great because the light is perfect for filming. Cheaper labour, too. It's a win win.'

So he's got a villa in Spain. Why am I not surprised?

'Come into the annex, it's where I keep my favourite things.' He held open the door. The walls were covered with photos of two naked women. They could have come from the pages of a porno magazine – and probably did. One was blonde, the other a brunette; absolutely nothing was left to the imagination.

'Just two of the models I used to work with... do they bother you?'

She tried to keep her eyes off them, preferring instead to take in the firearms displayed in a series of glass cabinets. 'I'm more interested in these...'

'They cost me a lot less than those gold-diggers...'

He pointed out an MP40 submachine gun, a German infantry weapon from World War 2: 'Do you know what this is?'

'Maschinenpistole vierzig.'

'I'm impressed. And you speak German?'

'Natürlich. And French. My Russian isn't too bad, either. Do they all work?'

'Of course... and I've got ammo for them as well. What about this one?'

'That's a Browning Hi Power, looks like a wartime FN model.' In the Corps, she had put more than a few rounds through one exactly the same, but decided to keep that to herself.

'You're very well informed for a woman.'

'No, just very well informed.'

He reached for a marble ashtray, stubbing out his cigarette with a hard, screwing motion. His eyes bored into her: 'You know, I can do you a lot of good.'

'Isn't it time we had some lunch?'

'I'd rather see what's under that trouser suit.' He stepped forward and pinned her against the wall. She brought her knee up, but he twisted round and took the blow against his right thigh.

'I expected you to fight, baby. And you know what? That just turns me on even more.'

His hands sliced inside her jacket. They didn't wander – he knew exactly where he wanted to put them. When he managed to plant a kiss, the taste of his last cigarette only added to her revulsion.

She continued to resist. By putting one foot against the wall she managed to get enough leverage to push him away – just far enough to launch a straight right. Her punch was packed with venom, but she over-committed. He parried and, in a classic jujitsu move, threw her over his shoulder.

She landed squarely on her back, her fall broken somewhat by the deep pile carpet. Now he was on top of her – and looking incredibly pleased with himself. His right hand was at her throat, the other tugging at the zip of her trousers. Again he forced his lips against hers. She twisted and turned, all the while looking for something that could deliver a knockout blow. She eyed the ashtray. It was only a few feet away, but she was unable to reach it. Then the phone rang.

'I think you'd better answer that.'

'Why should I when we're having so much fun?'

13

'I'm pretty sure it's Sandy. And if you stop rushing me, I'll give you what you want – and more.' She was making an offer his sex-obsessed ego couldn't refuse.

'I'll hold you to that in every possible way.'

'You might not have the energy.'

He got to his feet with a massive smirk on his face. She waited until he picked up – there was an extension in the annex – before retrieving her handbag. She had already decided that, if it was anyone other than Johnson on the other end, Arnold would be wearing that ashtray like a hat.

'Hi... Sophie said it would be you. I've just been showing her around.'

'And I've seen quite enough!' She said it loud and proud. 'If he tries to put the phone down, Sandy, call the police.'

As Arnold struggled to smooth things over, she adjusted her clothing and walked out. The tyres of her Saab kicked against the gravel drive just as he rushed out to deliver his parting shot: 'I don't need you!'

'You're breaking my heart,' she said, half under her breath.

She wasted no time in turning onto the B road that snaked back through the village. The sun was strong, and strobed through the maple trees as she drove along. She reached inside her jacket for her sunglasses. They were broken. And the top buttons were missing from her white satin blouse. She checked her wristwatch – it was still ticking, undamaged. Tough as she was, her knees were shaking. She'd had to fend off a few amorous drunks in her time, and not just from the lower ranks. But Arnold was pure sexual predator.

'Village Tea Rooms' said the sign up ahead. It was next to the post office, which had a call box outside. She called Johnson, who was suitably contrite: 'What can I possibly say?'

'Have you any idea what you sent me into?'

'Tony has apologised – '

'Apologised? He ought to be arrested.'

'Good thing Georgie insisted I called...'

'That girl's a treasure. I owe her big time.'

'Did he – ?'

'Get his wicked way with me? I'd have killed him first.'

14

'I feel so bloody awful...'

'I'm not blaming you, Sandy. Besides, he's moving to Spain soon anyway. Good riddance is all I can say.'

'You don't have to come back to the office... there's nothing spoiling here.'

'I'd rather do my job. That's what I'm paid for, isn't it?'

'Not after something like this – I feel as guilty as hell. Get back home as quickly as you can. You'll miss the traffic if you set off now.'

'I'm right by a tea shop. I think I'll have a good strong cuppa first.'

There was plenty of room to sit down. After all, it was a Monday, so the place wasn't exactly jumping. Most of the women seemed to be refugees from the Chelsea Arts Club. They also belonged to the stockbroker set, all cut-glass accents and designer labels. Some were on their second or third husband. Being traded-in for a younger model had its compensations, mostly in the form of a generous divorce settlement. They paid scant attention to Sophie, and carried on with their cream teas and conversation. The young waitress in the frilly white pinny behind the counter was much friendlier: 'Hello there. What would you like?'

'A pot of tea, please.'

'Any particular blend?' There were at least half a dozen alternatives chalked up on the board behind her.

'Something strong… something I can stand the spoon up in.'

The waitress smiled. 'I think you'll find our Assam fits the bill. I'll bring it over for you.'

Another customer arrived. She was not exactly surprised to see it was Sam. He came over to her table at the back of the room.

'Have you been following me? Not that I mind particularly. It's good to see you again.'

'Here we are,' said the waitress, removing a pot of tea and a cup and saucer from a wooden tray. 'Help yourself to milk and sugar.'

'My friend would like to order something.'

'I would?'

'You can hardly just sit there.'

'Coffee, black.'

15

'We have a selection,' said the waitress, giving him the menu. He glanced at it and ordered an Ethiopian.

Sophie put two sugars in her cup and poured. The tea was hot and she blew across the cup before taking a sip. 'That's the last time I visit him.'

'Your top buttons are missing.'

'My knees have only just stopped knocking – he went for me.'

'One Ethiopian,' said the waitress, unloading her tray. He added two cubes of sugar and gave the cup a gentle stir.

'Sympathy isn't your strong point, is it?'

'You seem to have recovered pretty well.'

'This tea isn't doing any harm – it's lovely. Where did you come from by the way? I didn't spot you on the road...'

'I parked up in the village. I knew you'd have to come back this way.'

'That was very astute of you, but why come all this way? How did you – ?'

'I wanted to have another look at Arnold's place. Impressive, isn't it?'

'Not impressive enough it would seem. He's moving to Malaga. And no, I'll not be visiting him over there.'

'What if I told you that he's setting himself up as an illegal arms dealer, bankrolled from Eastern Europe? We need to make sure his plans never come to fruition.'

'He's into guns, alright – I've seen his collection. But why would he get into that sort of thing? He certainly doesn't need the money.'

'I thought he might have mentioned something – or someone – that might be of interest.'

'The only person of interest to Arnold is himself.'

'Wouldn't you like to get even with him? All I ask is that you listen. And for that we need privacy, okay?'

'Not until you tell me who you are.'

'I'm a cultural attache... for the Embassy of Israel.'

'So you're a diplomat?'

'That's what it says on my accreditation.'

'Then why aren't you busy promoting tourism or something?'

'My role is more... political.'

16

'Then shouldn't you be sharing this with someone in British intelligence?'

'My boss thinks I already am. You have the right background, the right credentials – '

'You couldn't be more wrong. I hardly have the mental equipment for that sort of thing.'

'Do you really expect me to believe that?'

'Look – I've had one hell of a day, okay? All I want to do now is drive home, raid the fridge for some wine and have an early night.'

'I wouldn't blame you for doing that, for sure. But there's a place near here where you can rest up – perhaps you'd like to stay for dinner? The housekeeper's a brilliant cook.'

She didn't want to say yes too quickly, even though she was going to anyway. If anything the danger of the unknown made him even more intriguing. With Arnold the sex threat was implicit. Sam was smooth, and infinitely more likeable. 'What sort of place is it, exactly?'

'It's one of the perks of being a diplomat. It's comfortable, secluded.'

'And there's a housekeeper?'

'Helen. She can be your chaperone.'

'Can I follow you in my car?'

'For sure – the house isn't very far from here.'

She hadn't quite finished her tea, and decided to probe a little: 'Do you mind me asking how long you've been married?'

'Ah yes, the ring. We had three good years. Then one day Sarah went down to the beach with some friends. I kissed her goodbye at the bus stop outside our apartment in Tel Aviv. A terrorist came out of the sea with a machine-gun. She never came back. We had plans to settle down in a small village outside the city. She wanted to have kids...'

'I'm so sorry...'

'Afterwards all I wanted was revenge – that's why I applied for the special forces. I had this crazy notion I might get lucky and take out the guy who did it.'

'When you were in the pool, I couldn't help noticing –'

17

'My shoulder? It happened on a raid. My body armour took the first bullet. The second one sneaked past, but not before my radio mic had taken the sting out of it. I was lucky, for sure. Shall we go?'

Segev started his Golf and set off steadily, without racing through the gears. After they'd driven about five miles, the Golf turned up a tarmac driveway that curved behind a large stand of beech trees. He stopped to activate the automatic security gate, then drove on until she could see a large Edwardian house, brick built, set in several, well-tended acres. The front door was slightly ajar. She felt his hand on her shoulder as they went in. Helen Logaris hardly conformed to Sophie's mental image of a housekeeper. She was in the lobby, arranging flowers in a vase with care and precision.

'Former Olympic fencer,' said Segev.

After finding room for the last carnation, she took off her gloves and walked over to greet them. 'That was a long time ago, Sam.'

He introduced her: 'This is Sophie...Sophie Zoborski.'

'Shalom, Sophie. I'm Helen.'

They clasped hands. She had rather piercing hazel eyes and long black hair, worn up in a top knot. She was as trim as a cheetah. Sophie found it difficult to guess her age: it could have been anywhere between 30 and 40.

'What's happened to your blouse?' she asked.

'Bit of a wrestling match earlier. Not to Olympic standards, I'm afraid.'

'Are there any spare buttons attached?'

'I'm not sure to be honest. All I really need is a safety pin.'

'We can do better than that. Come on through to the study. We don't want you stripping off in front of this young man, do we?'

'I can take a hint,' he said.

Logaris pulled out a sewing box from the bottom drawer of a drum chest. 'If I could have your blouse...' Sophie undid the remaining buttons and handed it over.

'I wish my complexion was as good as yours, said Logaris. 'You have such a lovely tan.'

'I could say the same about you – must be all that swimming in the sea and warming back up on the beach afterwards.'

18

Logaris held up a strip of shell buttons: 'What about these? They're slightly creamier...'

'They look fine to me.'

She snipped off the remaining buttons before sewing on a new set. Sophie put the blouse back on, then walked over to a large, elaborately framed mirror. She untwisted the collar and flicked her hair back. 'As good as new – no one would know the difference.'

'There are three left over – you might as well have them. You never know when they might come in handy.'

Segev came back in, pausing in the doorway. She spoke to his reflection: 'Helen's a dab hand with a needle, too.' They heard a car pull up. 'That will be the boss.'

As he went to the front door, Sophie put the buttons in her handbag. Shortly afterwards, he re-entered the study with Berkowitz. 'So this is the young woman you've been telling me so much about.'

'Hello,' said Sophie.

'Let's have a little talk, shall we?' said Berkowitz.

She took a seat on the sofa next to Segev, and Logaris slipped away. Berkowitz took the armchair off to her left. The ornate clock on the mantelpiece chimed the quarter hour. Berkowitz opened his briefcase and took out a plain manilla file. 'Would you mind confirming a few details for me?'

'What kind of details?'

'By the way she's staying for dinner.'

'Excellent. Helen rarely disappoints. Details like your date of birth, for instance.'

'Twenty-sixth of March, Nineteen Forty-Nine.'

'And your service number is eight-nine-eight-two-three-five-four-two.'

'Who gave you that?'

'We have our sources.'

'Do you doubt my identity or something?'

'Not anymore, no.'

'Then what's the point of all this? I've already told Sam what happened with Tony Arnold.'

'He attacked her.'

19

'Interesting,' said Berkowitz. 'You appear to be remarkably resilient.'

'I think I'm losing my appetite. I don't really see much point in continuing, do you?'

'I'd rather you did. Tell me about your father, Dominik Zoborski.'

'What's there to tell?'

'He was born in Warsaw on the third of April, Nineteen Twenty-Five, was he not? And he fought in the war?'

'Dad doesn't talk about it very much.'

'Dominik Zoborski was a brave man. All honour to his name and memory. But he's not your father.'

'That's ridiculous. Of course he is.'

'Sergeant Dominik Zoborski DCM was murdered by the NKVD on the tenth of July, Nineteen Forty-Five.'

'You must have mixed him up with someone else.'

'We don't make mistakes like that. And did you know your mother had a sister?'

'She didn't. She was an only child, like me.'

'We tracked her down a few days ago. Her name is Drusilla Williams. At first she was very reluctant to talk about your father – they haven't spoken since your mother was killed.'

'It was an accident...'

'Mrs Williams believes your mother, Elizabeth, could have been murdered. Your father's real name is Albert Grobinski, born fifteenth of August, Nineteen Twenty-Six in Breslau – now Wrocław – in south-western Poland. And he certainly didn't stand with the Allies. Instead he was one of the many ethnic Germans who fought with the Wehrmacht.'

'Where did you get all this?'

'The truth is,' continued Berkowitz, 'that Grobinski became an agent of the Soviet intelligence service.'

'Do you seriously expect me to believe that?'

'Mrs Williams told us that Elizabeth loved to hang out with American servicemen. She was often on the quayside at Liverpool docks when troop ships were leaving for the States. According to your aunt, she was there when Grobinski arrived, and literally bumped into him. He'd been given Zoborski's identity by the NKVD.

'He was given instructions to blend in with the Poles who had decided to remain in Britain. Stalin had wanted every single Pole to be repatriated, but to their credit your government refused, knowing that anyone they sent back would probably be executed or shipped off to Siberia. Grobinski was spared because of his strong resemblance to Zoborski: he was about the right age and shared the same physical characteristics. Casualties among the Polish Second Corps were heavy, and only a handful of men from his battalion survived to settle in England. Your father avoided reunions anyway. Ever wondered why he preferred to speak English?'

'That's hardly surprising, is it?'

'I'll give you that. It made it easier for him fool the Polish community in Leicester. They admired him for bringing you up on his own. No one suspected he was an agent.'

'Dad told me all his family were dead. He told me the Poland he left behind no longer existed.'

'He could still be active. The Russians are keen to identify anyone sympathetic to the Solidarity movement. I can understand why he would want to save his skin at the end of the war... Zoborski's refusal to work with the new communist regime cost him his life. But when he got to England, your father could have turned himself in. Instead, he remained loyal to Moscow.

'At the inquest the coroner recorded a verdict of "Unlawful killing", yet the police failed to charge anyone in connection with your mother's death – something your aunt regards as unforgivable. It seems your father's impressive "war record" counted in his favour. The coroner even praised him for being "so stoic and upright".'

'The implication being...?'

'I'm just trying to help. You can drive away if you want. No one's stopping you.'

Segev made a suggestion: 'Why not speak to her yourself? We can go and see her together... it's up to you.' She looked him straight in the eye, but didn't speak.

'Perhaps you'd like something to drink?' suggested Berkowitz.

21

Segev left the room for barely a minute, and returned with a bottle of red wine. He brought the first glass over to her.

'I feel like throwing this in your face.'

'That would be a terrible waste,' said Berkowitz. 'It's Petite Sirah, from the Judean Hills.'

She heard a car starting up outside. It was the V8 of a Mercedes S-class.

'Please accept my apologies, I have to leave now. Enjoy your wine, Sophie.'

She drank freely. The wine was superb, and it was going down a lot better than what she'd heard from Berkowitz. She went to the window and watched as the Mercedes drove away. It was black with dark tinted windows and diplomatic plates.

Logaris re-entered the room, then came over and squeezed her hand: Sophie had never been touched quite like that, woman to woman.

'I've a lot to think about,' she said.

'You probably want to get home, but you're more than welcome to stay here. And you need to eat something.'

When Segev rejoined them, her glass was nearly empty. 'Can I top you up?'

'Why not? I may even forget this ever happened.'

'By the way, we won't be driving all the way – only as far as the airfield at Fairoaks. We have a helicopter there, a Hughes 500. It could land here, but we prefer not to attract attention.'

'I've been in a few helicopters in my time.'

'That makes two of us. You'll like the 500 – it's a fast machine.'

'Would you like to see your room... perhaps have a lie down?' suggested Logaris.

'Shall I take you up?' Segev gestured with an open hand.

'Lead on,' said Sophie.

'Okay with your drink?'

'I think I can manage.'

They went upstairs to one of the guest rooms. Everything was of the highest quality. She ran her hands lazily through the blue velvet curtains.

'I wish my flat looked like this. Not much of a view, though. Unless you like trees.'

Segev came over and placed his hand very lightly on the small of her back: 'Our diplomats and other VIPs stay here.'

'Do you mind if I take off my shoes?'

'You're our guest. Make yourself at home.'

'Is the bedroom through there?' She took the lead. He followed.

'This is lovely.' She sat on the edge of the bed. He took this as his cue to go back downstairs. But she hadn't quite finished with him – not yet.

'What did she look like?'

'You mean Sarah?'

'Tell me something about her.'

'Later, after dinner.'

'Tell me now.'

'She was beautiful... hair as black as the heavens. Blue eyes... she was a bit shorter than you.'

'I'll be more comfortable without this.' She held out her jacket and he put it on a hanger in the wardrobe. She drained her glass.

He held out his hand. 'Let me take that for you.'

'Come and sit next to me – I don't bite.'

He read the signal and kissed her on the lips. She sustained the contact and it became deeper, more sensual. She could feel the middle finger of his left hand tracing her spine – downwards. He did it slowly, and with just the right amount of pressure. She would have allowed him to go further, but it was a case of wrong time, wrong place. So she broke away.

'It's not that I don't like you...'

'I understand. After all, we barely know each other.'

'You could come back to mine – to the flat – after we've visited Mrs Williams.'

'I'd like that. I'll call you for dinner. The bathroom's over there if you'd like to freshen up.'

She took a shower. At first the water was chilly, and the shock made her gasp. As it warmed up, she began replaying her clinch with Segev – Tony Arnold would be insanely jealous!

23

After stepping out and drying off, she decided to fluff up the pillows and get into bed. The peacefulness of her surroundings, combined with the wine and the scent of freshly-laundered linen, sent her into a deep sleep.

Chapter II

Moscow, 1.30pm, local time
'I'm here to see the General,' said Colonel Koslov.
The guard snapped to attention, then checked Koslov's ID. Satisfied, he gestured towards a green door marked 'K107'. Before Koslov could take another step, the door opened wide and the General appeared.
'Fetch my car.'
The guard came to attention again, then marched off.
The General was Nikolay Maxim Kubishev. Tall and clean cut, he cut a dash in a light brown check Italian suit. His designer gold framed spectacles did not come from any store in Moscow, either. Koslov threw up a salute.
'We can be more informal, Artem Alexey. Welcome to the KGB's First Directorate.'
Kubishev was one of the select few who were 'in' on the priceless intelligence provided by 'Cobalt', the KGB's most important agent in America – or anywhere else for that matter. Cobalt had delivered the entire contents of Operation POWERPLAY to Moscow via the Soviet Embassy in Washington DC. Devised by Rear Admiral Gene Bullett, POWERPLAY ran to just fifteen closely typed pages. It was by no means the first plan for a pre-emptive strike against the Soviet Union, but it was the first – in theory at least – designed to avoid any risk of a counter-strike and the inevitable nuclear holocaust on home soil.
Bullett was no rabid escapee from the set of Stanley Kubrick's 'Dr Strangelove'. In February 1982, he'd attended a CIA presentation on the Soviet Union's stagnating economy. Growth had fallen below zero, and he feared any further decline could well be terminal. In the West, people queued for a hot theatre ticket or a movie. In the Soviet Union, people often had to queue for basic staples like bread or a decent cut of meat. Living standards were poor even compared to Eastern Bloc countries. The sheer abundance and variety of food products – not to mention consumer goods – enjoyed

by shoppers in the West was something those outside the Party elite could hardly imagine.

Despite limited attempts at reform, centralised planning and the cumulative effect of huge expenditure on both conventional and nuclear weapons had made the Soviet economy progressively weaker. And invading Afghanistan hadn't exactly helped. During World War 2, the United States had become a military and economic superpower. The Soviet Union could never be both, though by the 1970s its nuclear forces were more than capable of laying waste to Western Europe and North America.

Bullett believed that a superpower collapsing from within posed a grave threat to world peace and stability. As Soviet doctrine emphasised the early use of tactical nuclear weapons, the risk of escalation to a general exchange of strategic nuclear missiles – Armageddon – seemed obvious. POWERPLAY, he reasoned, presented a viable alternative. It was a contingency against a Soviet leadership prepared to bring the world crashing down around them.

Before arriving at the Pentagon, Bullett had commanded one of the first Ohio-class ballistic missile submarines. Sleek and nuclear-powered, they carried 24 Trident missiles armed with multiple nuclear warheads in the megaton range. It was the single most destructive war machine yet devised. Commanding the Gold Crew on board had been the pinnacle of his long career as a submariner. But that success had come at a price. The long months on patrol had seen his marriage descend to crush depth.

Until POWERPLAY was translated, the KGB had been unaware of 'Blue Diver', a top secret lightweight torpedo developed by the UK's Underwater Warfare Research Establishment. Unlike many of the defence projects run by the MoD, it had not experienced any cost-overruns or delays. That was not enough to save it from cancellation in yet another round of defence cuts. Those in the know at the Admiralty were particularly displeased. The British naval attache in Washington DC was asked if he knew anyone in the US Navy who might – on the basis of mutual interest – be willing to make the case for Blue Diver in the Pentagon.

Bullett was duly approached, and, after a private briefing, he went directly to the Secretary of State for Defense. Within days the US

Government had agreed to take over the entire programme. From that moment, Blue Diver went 'black'. The funding for it was hidden in the Fiscal Year 1982 budget among other US Navy weapons systems and research projects, something even the most forensically minded Senate committee would find difficult to spot.

After some initial huffing and puffing from certain members of the cabinet, Her Majesty's Government rubber stamped the decision on the grounds that it would be good for Anglo-American relations. Blue Diver was still on the secret list, and they expected it to stay secret, thereby avoiding any public debate on the matter.

Britain's best boffins had, inadvertently, given Bullett the game changer he'd been waiting for. POWERPLAY was predicated on eliminating the threat posed by the Soviet Navy's nuclear-powered ballistic missile submarines. Blue Diver's advanced array of sensors could not be fooled by noise-making decoys or other countermeasures. Crucially, it could also discriminate between different types of submarines – and not just by comparing their acoustic and magnetic signatures.

Blue Diver itself was difficult to detect. Its contra-rotating propellers were designed to make as little noise as possible, yet the torpedo was still capable of speeds in excess of 40 knots. In early trials against a Royal Navy diesel-electric submarine, the sonar operators in the sound room had commented on its eerie noise signature, not unlike that of distant whale song. Its warhead came with a shaped charge of high-performance conventional explosive that even a double-hull could not withstand. A maritime patrol aircraft or anti-submarine helicopter armed with Blue Diver promised to deliver exactly what Bullett needed – a guaranteed kill.

The US Navy already had the top secret Sound Surveillance System – SOSUS – which used hydrophones laid on the seafloor to detect and classify every Soviet submarine transiting the Greenland-Iceland-UK gap. Skilled operators based in the US and UK (in the latter case, from the Royal Navy), were able to 'cue in' hunter killer submarines, which then slipped in behind their unsuspecting prey, trailing them silently. Bullett also wanted the much larger torpedoes carried by these hunter killers to be retrofitted with Blue Diver's sensor package.

The missile silos protecting Soviet intercontinental ballistic missiles (ICBMs) had already been detected and pinpointed by US Hexagon reconnaissance satellites. So too had all their bomber bases. All would be attacked by Tomahawk cruise missiles, fired en masse to saturate the defences. Tomahawk was a new weapon which used a combination of GPS (also developed by the US Navy) and terrain comparison (TERCOM) technology to achieve the kind of accuracy that World War 2 bomber crews could only dream about. Bullett wanted production of Tomahawk to be ramped up massively. Simultaneous launching from submarines (using their torpedo tubes) as well as surface ships and B-52 bombers, would achieve the levels of overkill required. As for how many nuclear warheads would be needed, Bullett did not quote a specific number, only that it should be 'consistent with the assured destruction of all critical target groups'.

His Deep Strike strategy would also deal with other hardened targets such as command and control centres. Carrier-borne fighters and air force interceptors would be expected to shoot down any bombers that escaped obliteration on the ground. In addition to Tomahawk, another new weapon, the Lockheed F-117A 'Stealth Fighter', also promised to deliver its laser-guided Paveway bombs with unprecedented levels of precision.

From the moment the first Tomahawk found its target, the other members of NATO would be faced with a fait accompli: join the party or risk being attacked by Soviet tactical nuclear weapons. These were mobile (such as the new SS-20) and widely dispersed. Soviet surface ships and Warsaw Pact air forces in Eastern Europe could also be expected to deliver such weapons. Eliminating them would stretch NATO's resources to the absolute limit.

Bullett made no attempt to downplay the risks, recognising a Soviet mindset that in World War had simply refused to accept defeat. He expected any post-strike dialogue with the Soviet leadership to emphasise that no civilian areas had been targeted. Furthermore, NATO ground forces would remain behind existing borders. If – despite these assurances – the Red Army was ordered westwards, its massive tank armies would be supported by any tactical nuclear weapons that NATO had missed. The effect on West

Germany, let alone smaller countries such as the UK, Belgium and Holland, would be horrific. On the other hand, launching such an attack would leave Moscow and every other city in the Soviet Union at the mercy of America's massive nuclear arsenal.

Having discussed the implications of POWERPLAY, the General Secretary of the ruling Communist Party and his inner circle decided to act. The KGB's First Directorate had long been tasked with acquiring Western military technology through espionage – now it would be authorised to use more direct methods...

Kubishev and Koslov were walking purposefully down a long corridor illuminated by dome lights, all of which, Koslov noted, seemed to be working. And he could smell fresh paint – something he was hardly accustomed to. A glance inside the General's office had revealed furniture and fittings that looked practically new. The funding given to the Directorate was evidently quite generous.

As they stepped outside, it was late afternoon in Moscow. A black Volga was driven   into the quadrangle. Kubishev dismissed the driver and took the wheel himself. 'I preferred the Mercedes I had in Rome. This is like driving an old tractor.'

'Rome?'

'I was assigned to our embassy there for a few years. One of my better postings.'

They turned right onto the main road leading to Gorky Park. 'The Americans are never satisfied,' said Kubishev. 'They keep competing at every level, spending massively on their military in an attempt to break us.'

'We match them, though – don't we?'

'We have to recognise that we're reaching the limit of what we can do with the resources at our disposal. Which is why I've selected you to lead a special operation, one of the highest importance.'

'But why me, General? I'm hardly the Party's favourite boy.'

'Your flying ability and leadership qualities override everything. All other considerations are irrelevant. I've been authorised to initiate Operation VIKTOR – and you're the man to carry it out.'

Koslov had been seconded to the ostensibly civilian transport fleet, which was now operating a fortnightly cargo service into West

29

Midlands Airport. He had a rebellious streak the general liked – mainly because he thought it might be exploitable.

'Absolute secrecy must be maintained at all costs,' continued Kubishev. 'We'll only get one shot at this.'

'How much do you know about the investigation?' asked Koslov. 'Have you seen the accident report?'

'That hardly matters anymore. It's all in the past.'

'But have you seen it?'

'Of course I have – and your incautious letter to the commander-in-chief. You're lucky it wasn't passed on to someone less sympathetic.'

'I had to do something…'

'Would it help,' said Kubishev, his tone betraying more than a trace of irritation, 'if I made sure it was amended to your personal satisfaction?'

'You have that authority?'

'Of course – now just forget about it, Artem Alexey. Nothing less than the survival of the Motherland is at stake here. The next time you land in England, you'll be bringing back a new kind of torpedo, one that threatens the viability of our entire submarine fleet. It's absolutely imperative that we have this weapon – we simply don't have the time to develop our own version independently. We must act now.'

'What if they search the aircraft?'

'All they will find is your duty free scotch whisky. The actual pick up will be from a disused airfield between the airport and the coast. We've already identified two or three good landing sites, but the final choice will be yours. My deception plan to deal with English counter-intelligence is already progressing satisfactorily. You should have a clear run.'

'And if their air force tries to stop us?'

'They always shut down early on Friday afternoons, which is when you'll be picking up the package. And in any case, you won't be viewed as an intruder – not after your previous visits. I take it you're already comfortable with their air traffic control procedures?'

'We haven't had any problems so far... Major Shushkin's English is very good.'

'Which is another reason for optimism. I'm reliably informed their controllers are usually very helpful.'

'That's true, certainly.'

'So I'm not asking you to shit on the ceiling. You'll have all the support you need. I'm bringing in Captain Yuri Belyakov from the spetsnaz – he'll be your security officer.'

'Why do we need him? We were all checked out by the KGB before being selected for the flights to England.'

'Not by me personally. This mission is far too important to leave anything to chance.'

'I'll vouch for all of my crew. A few of the younger ones spend a bit more than they earn, but that hardly makes them defector material.'

'My information is that Lieutenant Yakovlev has been overly critical of our presence in Afghanistan – and of the system in general.'

'Then you might as well ground the lot of us. Replacing him would be unsettling for the rest of the crew – and he happens to be the best navigator on the squadron. If he's said too much, it's probably the vodka talking, nothing more.'

'I realise that morale is important...'

'Then please trust my judgement, General.'

'As you wish – but Belyakov stays. He's a fine officer, and he won't get in the way. Neither will Malenkovich, who'll be going along as an observer. Other comrades are already in position in England. They will bring the package to the airfield.'

Koslov bit his lip. Malenkovich was the unit's zampolit (political officer) and he would be an unwelcome presence.

'What do we know about the package? How heavy is it?'

'No more than four hundred kilogrammes, including the container. I know your An-12 will swallow it easily.'

'That means we can carry a full fuel load. We may need it.'

'You must be ready to go by Friday morning, without fail.'

'We are all patriots, General. We will not let you down. One last question – why VIKTOR?'

'It just happened to be the next codename on the list.'

Koslov drove his 4x4, a dark green UAZ-469, back to the checkpoint. In or out, security was tight. The guard's boots shone like mirrors and his AK-47 assault rifle was clean enough for a surgical procedure: 'May I speak with you for a moment, sir?'

'Go ahead, soldier.'

'This is the first opportunity I've had to thank you for saving my brother, Anatoly Vasily. We both know what the mujahideen do with prisoners.'

'It was my ass as well, you know.'

The guard smiled: 'It's been a true honour meeting you, Colonel.'

Koslov normally slept easily, but it was now two o'clock in the morning and he was still wide awake, staring at the bedroom ceiling. His nerves demanded a smoke, and he made to reach for a pack of cigarettes on the bedside table. Too bad he had actually given up years ago. His mind refused to settle as he tried to think of every angle, every contingency. He looked across at his wife, Olga, whom he had married in 1963. She was the meteorologist who had given him his first weather briefing when he reported for basic jet training at one of the many bases on the outskirts of the capital. She had borne him two fine sons, Artem Alekseyevich and Alexander Pavlev.

Artem had recently graduated from advanced flight training with glowing reports about his piloting ability. Like his father, he had finished near the top of his course, which virtually guaranteed a place among the crème de la crème of military pilots: those selected to fly supersonic fighters.

He recalled what his own father had said to him on graduation day: 'Not bad for the son of a foundry man!' He remembered the bear hug, the back slapping; the kisses on each cheek that kept coming, over and over. And he could see his dear mother, smiling and weeping at the same time, waiting for her turn. For years she had taken in washing to make ends meet, and waited for hours in long queues for bread and meat. No son of hers would ever go hungry.

Talent spotted at his local gliding club, Koslov won a place at a state-sponsored flying school. He soloed a piston-engine Yak-18 trainer after nine hours dual instruction, which is significantly better than average. A compact five-foot seven, he was the ideal height and build for the aircraft he would later fly in the frontline.

32

As he finally drifted off, his mind slipped into a dream world inhabited by a stream of happy memories. Soon he was back in the cockpit of his all-time favourite aircraft – the speedy MiG-21 jet fighter. With afterburner it was easily supersonic in level flight, yet he much preferred to sky dance, rolling and looping around clouds just for the sheer joy of it. Flying at high altitude, when all he could hear was the sound of his own breathing, had a serenity that was almost spiritual. He made sure his name was always on the list for every post-maintenance air test, weather check or any other flying duty he could finagle. For him, flying was the perfect escape from earthbound responsibilities, not to mention the state's relentless self-mythologisation.

His career progressed seamlessly from junior pilot to flight commander and, in August 1976, he was given command of a fighter regiment close to the East German border. He was a respected and popular leader, not least because he was always trying to get his pilots as much flying as possible.

A few months later he had greeted a new pilot, Lieutenant Dmitri Leonid Vasiliev, who had been sent from another MiG-21 unit with a report that spoke highly of his technical knowledge of intercept radars and his general flying ability. But within a few minutes of taking off, Koslov had found him out. Vasiliev had such poor situational awareness that he was a total liability in air combat. He even struggled to maintain basic formation, which is normally a given. His previous commander had decided to get rid of him with the simple expedient of a posting, a tactic used by air forces on both sides of the East-West divide.

Rather than pass the problem on to someone else, he decided to give Vasiliev a break. So he put down their names on the flight roster for a tactical formation refresher. Koslov's briefing for the sortie was calm, considerate and clear. He would not overload him; they would take off individually before joining up in swept battle formation. The new boy would have plenty of time to catch up, and then position himself about 200 metres to the right, and slightly behind, Koslov.

Koslov released the brakes, selected full afterburner, and felt his MiG surge forward. Soon he was accelerating through 500 kilometres per hour in a shallow climb. Then he cancelled

33

afterburner, leaving a smoky trail for Vasiliev to follow. Two minutes came and went. There was no sign of him – not until an unmistakable silhouette appeared above his cockpit. Instead of following instructions, Vasiliev was closing in from above, breaking a cardinal rule of formation flying. Before he could react, Koslov felt a sickening thud. The collision tore off the fin and rudder of his MiG, making it uncontrollable. His brain seemed to process what happened next in slow motion. He saw the other MiG, minus its left wing, rolling crazily towards the ground. Now he had only one thought: survival. His ejection seat worked perfectly; but his parachute snapped open only a second or two before he came down, awkwardly and heavily, in a potato field.

Two MiGs destroyed, one pilot killed, and another seriously injured. The subsequent investigation exonerated Vasiliev, whose uncle was a member of the Politburo. The possibility that his favourite nephew had screwed up had to be suppressed. Much to the disgust of his fellow pilots, Koslov was relieved of command. He was given the news in hospital, where he was being treated for a compound fracture of the spine. A visit from his typically overzealous political officer was the last thing he needed. He was in no mood for a tedious lecture about his duty to the state. It was probably just as well that he was incapacitated. But whether guilty or not, flying a fast jet was now out of the question. With his spine supported by metal pins, another ejection would, at best, mean a wheelchair for life. At least he was alive. The recovery team could find only the top of Vasiliev's skull (still inside his helmet), and a severed left foot, complete with flying boot. The rest of his body was never found; house bricks had to be added to his coffin to make up the weight.

It took over six months for Koslov to recover from a series of delicate operations, and a further three months to retrain as a transport pilot. Before the collision, tactical airlift had been the last thing on his mind. But when the offer was made – pilots with his experience were not exactly plentiful – he didn't need to think about it. After the sensitivity and speed of the MiG, flying the big Antonov An-12 was like steeple chasing a cow. Nevertheless he was pleased with his new aircraft. The alternative – flying a desk – was unthinkable.

Olga was pleased, too. She no longer worried about her husband when he set off for work each morning. Flying transports was inherently safer than being in the cockpit of a MiG. Yet, within a few short years, Koslov would see more danger than he could ever have imagined. In early 1980 he flew his first mission in Afghanistan. Even though his squadron was rotated from an airfield inside the Soviet Union, deployments to Bagram and other bases around the capital, Kabul, kept him away from home for months at a time.

As in other wars, those who flew were remote from the horrors below. The first reports of enemy contact confirmed that this was going to be a war of uncommon brutality. Russian prisoners could expect no mercy; torture and execution were routine. In retaliation little or no attempt was made to spare the lives of ordinary civilians; women and children, the old and the sick, were killed in village after village. Soviet forces were always vulnerable beyond the relative security of Kabul. As in Vietnam, helicopters were being shot down in large numbers, being relatively easy targets on or near their landing zones. The rebels, or mujahideen, controlled most of the countryside, and the consequences of being captured far from base were all too easy to imagine.

There were no railways and few major roads. The night belonged to the rebels, so everything had to be transported by day. Air transportation was inherently safer and more reliable. Koslov and his crew were kept busy flying troops and supplies out to rough, unprepared strips. The worst part was flying back laden with body bags. On the plus side, the mountains in the north were spectacular, and having a pair of reliable engines on each wing was reassuring.

The rebels had no air force; what they did have was plenty of heavy machine guns and small arms. They also had large numbers of rocket-propelled grenades – the dreaded RPG-7. This Soviet anti-armour weapon was highly prized by the rebels, and their mastery of it came as a nasty shock. But as altitude was gained, such threats receded.

Nonetheless, from time to time his crew had reported some extra ventilation in the fuselage from pot-shots taken when they were low and slow. The engineers usually managed to find the bullet holes and make repairs – usually a simple patch would suffice. It was soon discovered that some of the rounds were coming from British Lee Enfield bolt-action rifles, a perennial favourite with various Afghan tribes.

The holes became bigger on the day they were detailed for a medevac mission from an improvised strip near Kunduz in northern Afghanistan. A Red Army lieutenant in the paratroops was among the walking wounded, and his account of what happened was instrumental in Koslov being awarded the Order of the Red Banner for gallantry. With his aircraft raked by machine-gun fire, he had managed to take off despite the No 1 engine taking numerous hits and powering down. His skill in handling a heavily loaded aircraft in a critical situation had undoubtedly saved the lives of everyone onboard. He himself had recommended the two snipers in the rear guard, both of whom had been particularly brave. They had stayed outside until the last possible moment and picked off three rebels armed with RPG-7s. Pavlovich, manning the rear turret, had also opened up with his twin 23 millimetre cannons just as soon as he could bring them to bear. A few well-aimed bursts from him suppressed any further opposition.

Before he finally managed to get some sleep, Koslov had concluded that, although this new mission had its risks, they hardly included being tortured and killed. If they were captured, the English would most likely offer them a cup of tea.

Chapter III

Segev came back to wake Sophie about half an hour before dinner. 'Have I been asleep for long?'

'Just a couple of hours.'

She stifled a yawn: 'That wine must have gone to my head...'

'Come down whenever you're ready.'

Logaris certainly knew how to cook. They dined on creamy roasted garlic and potato soup, grilled salmon fillet with honey mustard sauce, and classic coffee cake.

'That was wonderful,' said Sophie.

Segev agreed. 'She spoils us all.'

'It's getting late,' said Logaris, 'and you need to be up early in the morning.'

Logaris walked over to the baby grand piano next to the window. 'Would you like a nightcap, Sophie?'

'Do you mean a musical one?'

'What would you like me to play?'

'I don't know...'

'What about some Chopin?' suggested Segev.

'It's Sophie's choice.'

'That's okay by me.'

'In that case we'll have one of his nocturnes, opus nine, number two in E flat major.'

Her playing was sublime. For the next four minutes or so the music transcended all other thoughts and feelings. When the last note faded away, Sophie applauded enthusiastically: 'That was amazing – it really was – what a talent you have!'

'Paris Conservatoire,' said Segev.

'I'm glad you liked it,' said Logaris, closing the lid of the piano.

Segev went up with Sophie; they parted company at the top of the stairs. 'Layla tov.'

'I take it that means goodnight...'

'Sleep well. I'll see you in the morning.'

After breakfast, they sped off through what remained of the early morning mist. There was hardly any traffic and they arrived at Fairoaks just as the helicopter was being pushed out of the hangar. Sophie went to find a phone. She called the office.

'Good morning, Sandy Johnson Associates...'

'It's me.'

'Sophie! How are you?'

'I'm fine, honest, Georgie. I just need to speak to Sandy.'

'Putting you through... look after yourself.'

'Thanks.'

'I've been expecting a call from you,' said Johnson.

'I'm really sorry about this...'

'You're sorry? I went round to your flat last night with champagne and roses.'

'I decided to stay near Kingly Brook.'

'Oh...?'

'I might be away for a day or two.'

'I'll keep the champers in the fridge. Georgie's put the roses in a vase.'

'You're a sweetie. By the way, the Saab is amazing.'

'I knew you'd like it.'

'I'm leaving it at Fairoaks for the time being. I'll explain everything later.'

Assisted by a healthy tailwind, they touched down at Speke Airport, Liverpool, barely 1 hour 20 minutes after lifting from Fairoaks. When they emerged from the art deco terminal building, Segev hailed a taxi. 'Twenty-seven Olympic Avenue.'

The driver didn't say much. He probably felt inhibited by Segev, though that didn't stop him from eyeing up Sophie in the rear view mirror. But he managed to keep at least one eye on the road.

They pulled up outside a well-kept, mid Thirties terraced property. Sophie got out first, paid the driver, and let Segev lead the way. The cast iron gate clattered back against the latch. By the time they got to the front porch, Drusilla Williams was standing in the doorway. 'Oh love!' she gushed. 'You're your mum's double! Step inside before I embarrass myself in public.'

'Come straight through,' she continued, beckoning them into the living room. 'Let me have a proper look at you... you're tall, like her... and just as pretty. Those high cheekbones... those beautiful brown eyes... all from your mum, they are.'

She hugged Sophie, then kissed her on both cheeks. Sophie did not kiss her back. She felt no kinship. On the contrary – she felt more than a little self-conscious.

'Good looks seem to run in the family.'

Segev had sensed Sophie's unease, though his tactful compliment was appreciated more by Mrs Williams. 'He's a charmer this one, isn't he?'

'Yes,' said Sophie, managing a thin smile.

'Sit yourselves down, then. I'll put the kettle on.'

From the settee she surveyed the various photographs displayed on the sideboard. Pride of place went to a wedding photograph in a silver frame of the new Mrs Williams and her clearly delighted groom. There was also a wonderful photo of Drusilla and Elizabeth walking arm-in-arm along the promenade of a seaside resort, almost certainly Blackpool.

Mrs Williams re-emerged with a tray laden with a teapot, cups and saucers, milk jug, sugar bowl and a large biscuit barrel. 'It needs to brew a bit longer,' declared Mrs Williams, adjusting the tea cosy. 'There's nothing worse than weak tea, if you ask me.'

'That's a beautiful tea service,' said Sophie.

'Crown Derby. Gordon bought it for us after his first big promotion.'

'I've been admiring your wedding photo.'

'Good looking fella, isn't he? I did well there. My dress was old and borrowed all in one. It was very much make-do-and-mend in those days. None of us had any money to spare – people just rallied round.'

'How did you meet?'

'Well, one day Gordon came into the typing pool at work. He asked if anyone was available for a rush job. My supervisor called my name and I looked up. I was fast, you see, sixty or seventy words a minute. He smiled at me and I smiled back. I sort of knew I'd end up marrying him, though it took him a fortnight to pluck up the courage to ask me out.'

'I suppose that wasn't a bad job in those days...?'

'A lot better than being on the dole – I can tell you that for nothing, pet. I was determined to better myself, as we used to say. After the war all the blokes wanted their old jobs back, so us girls doing factory work were given the bum's rush. I learnt shorthand on a correspondence course and joined Hall Engineering in Speke because that's where I was sent by the bloke in the Labour Exchange.'

'What did your husband do?'

'He'd always been mechanically minded – rebuilding old motorbikes, that sort of thing – but didn't do much at school. He landed on his feet in the RAF doing his national service. They trained him up as an airframe fitter. That stood him in good stead when he came out, because he was able to walk straight into a job over at Squires Gate making Hunter jets. When that job finished he went over to Hall Engineering, because like everyone else they badly needed skilled men. Triumph's took us over, and Gordon ended up as a production engineer on the TR7.'

'Hasn't that factory closed now?'

'Hasn't it just! They locked the gates in Seventy-Eight and threw away the key. Gordon said the management were as much to blame as the blokes down on the line. They had the worst absenteeism and productivity in the whole of Leyland – and that's saying something. That's why he's working out in South Korea. He said it was like a dream come true – total cooperation, no strikes, no stoppages. They all wanted to work. Sorry, pet. I've gone on a bit, haven't I?'

She poured out the tea. 'There's every biscuit known to man in there... just help yourselves.'

Sophie picked out a chocolate digestive, then pointed at the other photo. 'Is that you and mum in Blackpool?'

'That's Blackpool alright. That would've been taken in... let me think... Nineteen Forty-Three – wartime – and Liz would have been seventeen. She had two years on me, you see.'

'You're obviously enjoying yourselves...'

'We had three-eighths of bugger all... but we were happy. We lived in a two-up two-down in Toxteth. No one ever locked their doors and everyone felt safe – apart from when Jerry lobbed a few bombs at us. Liz loved to go out. She'd tell me all about the dances she'd been to and how so-and-so had tried it on a bit.'

'What else did she get up to?'

She loved going to the pictures. But then we all did. She had scrapbooks full of publicity shots of all the big stars. Tyrone Power was her absolute favourite. She loved to read, too. Went through books like no tomorrow, two or three every week. She was a bright girl, our Liz...'

'Do you think my Dad was involved in her death?'

'You don't stand on ceremony, do you, pet? It just seemed impossible for her to just go like that when she had so much to live for... but then I'm not exactly impartial, am I? She was my beautiful big sister, and I loved her to bits.'

'Dad's always been good to me. He's never lifted a finger against me. He's always helped me, encouraged me...'

Mrs Williams became tearful: 'I'm sorry... I knew this would happen... I knew it would...'

'I didn't come here to upset you, believe me.'

'I know, pet. Sorry about the waterworks. I've got some more photos upstairs.'

She returned with an old biscuit tin, which she handed to Sophie. Inside were about twenty black and white photos; some were creased or faded – or both. A few near the bottom of the pile were in much better condition. Sophie selected just one. It was a head and shoulders portrait of a man in uniform – clearly American – of the type used in a security pass. On the back, written in pencil, was the name 'Todd'.

'Where did this come from?' asked Sophie.

'It came with the others... Dominik sent them to me a few months after the funeral.'

Sophie put the photo back in the tin. 'Thank you for your hospitality, Mrs Williams. I –'

'For goodness sake call me Drus – everyone else does.'

'I think it's time we were going.'

41

'Can't you stay a bit longer?'

'I'm afraid not. Duty calls.'

'Before you go, there's something you might be able to help me with. I've never said anything about it to anyone. I'll just go and fetch it – it won't take a minute.' She returned clutching a battered leather briefcase. 'It's a bit dusty... I only took it out of the loft yesterday. It's not been opened since Liz passed away. When we moved I meant to chuck it in the Mersey...'

She handed the briefcase to Segev. The lock was broken, so he needed only to unbuckle the two straps. He reached inside and pulled out a dark brown leather holster. He opened the flap and withdrew a semi-automatic pistol.

'*Russian?*' asked Sophie.

'For sure,' said Segev. 'Tokarev TT-33... 7.62 millimetre... a real life-taker.' He reached back into the case and found a pair of 8-round box magazines and a cleaning kit. 'It's all here.'

'Can I have a look?'

Before handing it over, he operated the slide and checked the firing chamber. 'It's safe.'

She cradled the weapon, examining it thoroughly. 'Date stamped Nineteen-Forty-Four... it appears to be as good as new.'

She operated the slide, then checked the half-cock notch on the hammer. 'That's interesting... there's no safety catch.'

'How come you know so much about these things?' asked Mrs Williams.

'The gun club in Germany.'

'There's no need for you to keep this,' said Segev. 'Let me take it off your hands.'

'I should've thrown it in the Mersey years ago. Why Gordon wanted to keep it, I'll never know.'

Sophie had seen and heard quite enough for one day. A tearful Mrs Williams waved furiously from the front gate as the taxi pulled away.

'We need to change this,' said Segev, looking at the dilapidated briefcase. 'It might attract the wrong kind of attention.'

'He spoke to the driver: 'Where I can buy a briefcase?'

'There's a WH Smiths comin' up on the right... will that do for you?'

'Perfect... then go straight to the airport.'

'Just so long as you know the meter's runnin', like.'

Segev entered the shop. It wasn't busy and he returned a few minutes later with a black attaché case. As they drove away, he tried to transfer the Tokarev. The lid of the new case wouldn't close. 'It must be the holster,' she whispered. 'It's too bulky as it is – let me help you.' She put the case on her lap and held it open. He withdrew the pistol from the holster. He was just about to place it inside when the taxi lurched violently to one side and performed an emergency stop. The case slid off her knees in an instant. Segev was now holding the pistol in plain view.

'That gormless bitch just stepped out in front of me!' exclaimed the driver, referring to the young mum who, without bothering to look, had pushed her buggy into the road. She was smoking a cigarette. Her baby was fast asleep. He opened the window and shouted: 'Your death wish is gonna come true if you carry on like that!' Then he saw Segev sliding the pistol under his jacket. He'd hidden it as quickly as he possibly could – but not quickly enough. 'That's a gun isn't it, mate?'

'There's no need to be concerned,' said Sophie. 'It's only a relic from the war – we're taking it to a private collector.'

'Whatever you say, love.'

She retrieved the case and they tried again. He put everything inside and she closed the lid. But while they had been stationary, a public-spirited pedestrian had also spotted the gun. He dialled 999 from a phone box.

'Nine-nine-nine emergency, which service do you require?'

'Police... there's a man with a gun.'

'Did you say a gun?'

'That's right, love.'

'What kind of gun?'

'A pistol... it looked like an automatic to me.'

'Can I take your name, please?'

'Garside... Derek Garside.'

'What number are you calling from?'

43

'Someone's vandalised the card, but I'm in the High Street, Speke, just up from the post office.'

'Can you describe the gunman?'

'Not really – he was in a taxi – but I did see him point the gun at the driver.'

'Can you remember the registration?'

'I know it ended in a "K"… it was a proper black cab, like, not a minicab.'

'Stay where you are, please. Officers will be with you shortly.'

Ten seconds later, a telephone was ringing at the nearest Merseyside Police station. 'B Division, WPC Keeley...'

'Is that you, Karen?' asked Chief Superintendent David Matthews. 'Yes – it's me, sir.'

'We need some officers with firearms, fast. A member of the public has reported a man with a gun in the back of a taxi on High Street, Speke. Could be a false alarm, but we have to play it safe. Tell your guv'nor to get a move on.'

'Guv,' said Keeley, turning towards Detective Inspector Vince Copeland, 'we need firearms right away.'

'What we got, gorgeous?'

'Man with a gun in a taxi, guv – last seen on Speke High Street.'

'Who else is current on firearms?' he asked.

'Just Kev – he's helping out on the front desk,' replied Detective Sergeant 'Mac' MacDonald.

'He's Butch and I'm Sundance,' said Copeland. We'll draw a couple of thirty-eights.'

The two men pushed back their chairs, and MacDonald darted out of the office. Copeland shouted after him: 'Tell Kev I'm on my way.' He patted Keeley on the shoulder. 'Be ready to put the kettle on when we get back.' She was young – 19 years old – and he had a soft spot for her.

'It's been a while since we had these out,' said PC Kevin Stevenson as they signed for two .38 Smith & Wesson Model 36 revolvers, together with twenty-four rounds of ammunition.

'What do we know, guv?' asked Stevenson, as he quickly stuffed the spare rounds into his trouser pocket.

'Could be something or nothing,' replied Copeland. 'But it's time we weren't here.'

Copeland was blowing hard by the time they got into their unmarked Ford Grenada. He had joined the force in 1959 after spending a year in the army on national service. He was much fitter then, of course. Apart from the added timber caused by too many fry ups and too little exercise, he was paying the price of a cigarette habit he had no desire to kick. He also drank too much. The top drawer of his office filing cabinet usually had a bottle of scotch in it.

'Go like fuck,' he said, still gasping.

MacDonald revved the engine to the red line. When they were up to 45 miles per hour in second gear, he kept the hammer down in third as the first update came in over the radio.

'Charlie Hotel to X-ray...'

Copeland picked up the handset, cleared his throat, spat out the window, and keyed the button: 'This is X-ray, over.'

'We've been updated by officers at the scene... two suspects, a man and a woman, both smartly dressed. Man is medium build, dark hair, age about thirty-five, wearing dark brown jacket. Woman is slim, dark hair, light blue jacket...standby X-ray...just received via taxi controller...suspect vehicle is a London taxi, registration Kilo Mike Kilo, Eight Five Seven Kilo...destination could be the airport.'

'All received. Any update on the weapon?'

'Negative, Charlie Hotel out.'

'I wonder what's going on, guv?' asked Stevenson. 'It doesn't sound like a bank job.'

'Best not take any chances,' cautioned Copeland. 'Even if we don't see a gun, be ready for anything.'

'I'm well up for it guv,' replied Stevenson, with a mock bravado he hoped would disguise how nervous he really was. 'I could use a bifti, though... and I'm out.'

Copeland struggled to fish out a couple of cigarettes as MacDonald hustled the big Ford left and right through the traffic. Despite using the entire roadway he nearly collided with a dawdling pea green Morris Minor. It was being driven by a woman of pensionable age wearing horn rimmed spectacles, a twinset and pearls. She appeared to be totally unperturbed by the near miss.

45

'Stupid old bat!' shouted Copeland, as he managed to find the Zippo lighter in his jacket pocket. Finding it was one thing – lighting up was proving more difficult. 'Gimme a break, Mac! Keep the bloody thing straight, will you?'

'We're almost there, guv,' replied MacDonald.

'There they are!' shouted Stevenson.

Segev was just getting out of the taxi as Copeland and his crew swept in. The Ford came to a halt, tyres squealing, within inches of the taxi's front bumper. Copeland was out first, pistol drawn and aimed directly at Segev. Holding his warrant card aloft with his free hand, he called out a warning: 'Armed police... stay exactly where you are!' Now Stevenson had Segev in his sights also. 'I'm Detective Inspector Copeland, Merseyside CID. Don't move unless I say so.'

Segev had a Home Office permit to carry a firearm for self-defence, but had decided to travel without it. He hadn't expected to be in much danger in Liverpool. 'I'm unarmed,' he said, and began to open his jacket.

'I told you not to bloody move!' shouted Copeland. The tension was palpable. Trigger fingers were getting itchy. 'Now put your hands on the roof and spread your legs. And do it *slowly*.'

Segev complied. More police cars arrived, and, after a sweeping hand gesture from Copeland, the other officers ushered away the small queue at the taxi rank. This was his show and he was going to run it his way. 'Now, let's see who's with you.'

Sophie stepped out of the taxi and stood next to Segev. Her handbag and the attaché case were still on the back seat.

'Exactly the same, miss,' barked Copeland. 'Hands on the roof, legs apart.'

'She's fit, guv,' whispered Stevenson. As he re-adjusted his grip, the pistol nearly dropped from his hand. Copeland didn't miss much, and Stevenson raised his free hand apologetically.

'Shall I search them, guv?' asked MacDonald. Copeland nodded. It was pretty obvious that Sophie wasn't carrying anything, but he patted her down anyway. *Lucky bastard,* thought Stevenson. Segev was next. 'They're clean, guv.'

'Right, let's have some names,' said Copeland.

'Can we have a little privacy, sir?' asked Segev.

'No problem, son. We'll take you down the station for a cosy chat.'

'I don't think that will be necessary.' Segev was trying to negotiate a way out. 'I have –'

'I'll decide what's necessary, not you. Now get in the back of the car. Mac, you search the taxi.'

'You can get out now, mate,' said MacDonald, speaking to the taxi driver. 'We'll need a statement from you right away.'

'Alright, but I'm bustin' for a pee, like.'

'Be quick about it... my guv'nor isn't a patient man.' The cabbie headed straight for the toilets. MacDonald could see Sophie's handbag and the case on the back seat. The latter had a combination lock. The old briefcase was on the floor. He checked underneath the driver's seat as well – just to be on the safe side. Then he walked back to the Ford: 'We've got a white handbag, a black attaché case that looks brand new, and a battered old briefcase.'

'Okay,' said Copeland, addressing Segev from the front passenger seat, 'let's have it.'

'As I was trying to tell you, I have diplomatic immunity.'

'Do you now? What's your name?'

'Samuel David Segev.'

'You're not from this parish are you, son?'

'No… I was born in Nazareth.'

'Nazareth?'

'That's correct.'

'And what do you do, exactly?'

'I'm the assistant cultural attaché at the Embassy of Israel.'

'Are you now?'

'Yes.'

'And you can prove all of this?'

'For sure, sir. You'll find I'm accredited to the Court of Saint James.'

'The what?'

'The Court of Saint James. Just like all diplomats to this country.'

'So you're a diplomat?'

'That is correct.'

'I'm guessing you didn't come here for the weather?'

'We came to see my aunt,' said Sophie.

'And your name is?'

'Sophie Zoborski. I was born in Leicester.'

'Doesn't have quite the same ring as Nazareth does it, miss?'

'Not really. We can't choose where we're born though, can we?'

'I don't do philosophy, love. I'm a policeman.'

'I take full responsibility for what's in that case,' said Segev. 'I'm allowed to carry a weapon –'

'We'll see about that. Go and get the bloody thing, Mac... and use a handkerchief.'

'Guv.'

MacDonald brought it over. 'Let's see what we've got here,' said Copeland, who attempted to slide the catches. 'Locked. What's the combination, son?'

'I don't have to answer any more questions.'

'That's fine, we'll take it with us. Open the boot Mac, will you?' As they moved to the rear of the car, Segev got out. 'Where do you think you're going, sunshine?'

'Back to London.'

'Get back in the car,' snapped Copeland, almost snarling.

Segev reached into his inside jacket pocket: 'It's my embassy ID. I strongly advise you to check it before you go any further.'

Segev and Copeland were now facing each other, but not yet toe-to-toe. It was a standoff.

'No harm in calling Special Branch, is there, guv?' said MacDonald.

Copeland didn't answer immediately. What he really wanted to do was cuff Segev and stuff him back in the car. But MacDonald's counsel, and the obvious fact that Segev looked pretty useful, swayed his decision. He took his ID and looked it over. 'I'm not taking this as gospel.'

'Why not guv?' said Stevenson. 'He was born in Nazareth, wasn't he?'

Copeland didn't appreciate the wisecrack. He was in unfamiliar territory, and he knew it. He wasn't dealing with the usual low life he'd been locking up for years. MacDonald was trying to offer his old mate a way out. Copeland took it: 'Go on, then. Call 'em.'

'Not looking very good, is it?' said Sophie.

'We'll work something out,' replied Segev.

Copeland was unimpressed: 'If you think you can dictate the terms of this investigation, think again.'

'I've got Special Branch on the line. They'd like a word.'

MacDonald gave him the handset. 'DI Copeland...'

'This is DS Wakefield. I understand you might have a bod there with diplomatic immunity.'

'He's given me ID from "The Embassy of Israel" in the name of Segev... that's sierra-echo-golf-echo-victor... initials sierra delta.'

'Stand by... we're just checking the list...'

'That cabbie's taking his time,' said MacDonald.

'Where the bloody hell's he got to?' Copeland glanced at his wristwatch and lit another cigarette: 'He's been gone a good five minutes. Talk about taking the piss. Get the little bastard over here, and I mean right now.'

'Guv.'

'Hello? DI Copeland?'

'Copeland here – sorry about that, mate.'

'He's a diplomat alright. Just get him to confirm his date of birth.'

Copeland held out the handset: 'We need your date of birth.'

'Tenth of May, Nineteen Forty-Six.'

Copeland put the receiver back to his ear: 'Did you get that?'

'All copied,' replied Wakefield. 'I understand from Sergeant MacDonald that you think our man might have something he shouldn't. Is that correct?'

'We believe it's in a black attaché case.'

'He has a special permit for a Beretta automatic. Is that what's in the case?'

'I don't know – he won't give me the combination.'

'Is it marked as a diplomatic bag?'

'Not that I can see.'

'You can't detain Segev, or search his person. But it's your call as far as the case is concerned.'

'Thanks for that.'

'Off you trot,' said Copeland, talking to Segev but looking at MacDonald. He waited until Segev made a move towards the case. 'Oh no you don't – that stays with us, son.'

'It's my property, sir.'

'Not according to Special Branch. They've confirmed you're protected by diplomatic immunity, but the case isn't. I've reason to believe it contains an unauthorised firearm. So you have a choice – leave it with us, or give us the combination so we can all see what's inside. It's up to you.'

'Do what you want,' said Segev, 'I've had enough of this.'

'Haven't you forgotten something?' asked Copeland.

'Try one-two-three-four.'

'Will I see you later?' asked Sophie.

'Maybe,' said Segev, as he walked purposefully towards the terminal building.

'I'm not sure I like your boyfriend's sense of humour,' said Copeland. 'Anyone got a screwdriver?' He dragged hard on his cigarette as Stevenson returned with the taxi driver in tow.

'Is this gonna take long?' asked the cabbie.

'Where the fuck have you been?'

MacDonald brought round the toolkit from the boot. Copeland picked up the wheel brace. The cabbie looked worried: 'You're not going to use that on me, are you?'

'Don't tempt me.' Copeland attacked each lock in turn. 'Sometimes,' he continued, 'there's no substitute for brute force.' He lifted the lid.

'Looks like we've hit the jackpot, guv,' said Stevenson.

'That's the gun alright,' confirmed the cabbie.

'This is Harry Fisher,' said Stevenson. 'He's been driving for –'

'Spare me his bloody life story,' said Copeland. 'Just gimme the headlines.'

'Go ahead Mr Fisher,' said MacDonald in a friendly tone. 'You're not in any trouble… we'll take a full statement from you later, okay?' MacDonald was always the 'good cop' when he worked with Copeland.

'Well, I picked 'em up from Olympic Avenue in Speke.'

'Number twenty-seven, wasn't it?' said Stevenson.

50

'Spot on. Anyway, it was just a local job, like, straight to the airport. Well, that was until –'

'Until what?' Until you saw the gun?' said Copeland, in rapid-fire fashion. The headlines weren't coming fast enough.

'The bloke said he wanted to buy a briefcase, so I stops outside WH Smiths. He gets back in the cab and the next minute this dozy bird with a chavvy in a pram steps out in front of me. Well, I had to slam on the anchors, didn't I? That's when I saw it, in me rear view mirror, like.'

'Was he pointing it at you?' asked MacDonald.

'No.'

'Did he threaten you?'

'No.'

'Thank you, Mr Fisher,' said MacDonald. 'You've been very helpful.'

'One more thing,' said the cabbie.

'Get on with it, Columbo,' said Copeland, sharply.

'The bird said it was for a collector.'

Copeland gave the case to MacDonald, who put it in the boot. It was time to take stock. 'Where do we go from here, guv?'

'Back to the nick.' Copeland got out, then opened the offside rear door and sat next to Sophie. 'Have we got a firearms certificate?'

'No... I've never actually needed one.' She knew what was coming next. And that suited her just fine – she wanted to get away from there as quickly as possible.

'Let's go,' he said, flicking away his cigarette. 'You can ride in front, Kev. I'll look after the lady here.'

MacDonald got back behind the wheel and started the Grenada. After a neat bit of reversing, they were on their way.

'In case you didn't know,' said Copeland, 'you're under arrest. You don't have to say anything unless you wish to do so, but what you do say may be given in evidence. Do you understand?' He was already tapping another Park Drive on the packet.

'I'd rather you didn't smoke.'

He lit up anyway. At least he wound down the window a little before launching what for him amounted to a charm offensive. 'Why don't you tell me what's going on? If you're straight with me, I'll see what I can do.'

'It would be good to know what I'm being charged with.'

'Carrying a firearm in a public place. That'll do for now.'

'The music stopped, and I've ended up holding the parcel.'

'That's too bad,' he said, flicking the ash from his cigarette out the window. 'We don't see many birds like you in this job. What's the word I'm looking for, Mac?' he asked, clicking his fingers.

'Sophisticated?'

'Yeah... sophisticated.' MacDonald grinned. He parked up the Ford, and after the usual preliminaries at the front desk, she was led towards Interview Room 1.

'I'm allowed a phone call, aren't I?'

'There's one on the wall over there,' said Copeland. 'Be my guest.'

She didn't have a solicitor – that would not have been her first call anyway. With any luck her dad would be in the office. 'Hello – is Dominik Zoborski there?'

'Who's calling please?' asked his secretary.

'It's his daughter, Sophie.'

'He must be in a meeting. Can I take a message?'

'Not really. It's rather urgent.'

'Bear with me a moment...'

Copeland came over, pointing at his wristwatch. 'We haven't got all day, you know.'

'I think you're in luck, Sophie. I'll put you through.' Copeland was only a few feet away from her, drinking coffee from a plastic cup.

'I'd appreciate a little privacy, if you don't mind.'

'Just pretend I'm not here.'

'Hello, is that you Dad?'

'Is everything alright?'

'Not exactly. I'm in Liverpool... in a police station.'

'What are you doing there?'

'I saw my Aunt this morning, and things have kind of spiralled from there.'

'Oh no –'

'Don't be too hard on yourself. I wasn't that impressed with her, to be honest.'

'She thinks I –'

'We're being overheard, Dad, just so you know.'

'But what's happened to you?'

'There's been a bit of a misunderstanding, that's all. We'll talk more when I get home. I won't be here for much longer – hopefully.'

'Is there anything you want me to do?'

'No – just sit tight. I just thought I'd better let you know. By the way, I've got a present for you. I'll bring it over the next time I see you. It's a bit awkward to send in the post. You can probably guess what it is…'

'Time's up,' said Copeland.

'I have to go now, Dad. I'll come and see you as soon as I can. Don't worry, everything will be okay.'

Her father replaced the receiver. He looked at the framed photo he kept on his desk. There she was, beaming back at him on the day of her passing out parade. He held it up like a mirror. He could see the reflection of his own face superimposed on hers. *I should have told you about Drusilla a long time ago...*

Chapter IV

Following normal procedure, Special Branch had sent a message about the incident outside the airport, duly received at 11.37am by the duty officer at 140 Gower Street, the address of an unprepossessing ten-storey office block built in the 1950s. Within easy walking distance of Regent's Park, it was the London HQ of the Security Service (MI5). The message soon found its way to the sixth-floor office of MI5's Director General, Sir Stephen Sharp.

Sir Stephen certainly lived up to his name. He was also sharp sartorially. Suits and shirts from Savile Row, shoes by Lobb. He was recruited from the Grenadier Guards, having been approached while viewing Sumerian antiquities at the British Museum. He had read classics at Cambridge, and retained a keen interest in the study of ancient civilisations. Now 57, he lived in Henley-on-Thames with his wife, Felicity, in a substantial Georgian house by the river. The property, complete with four surrounding acres of landscaped gardens and a boathouse, had been left to him by his father, from whom he had also inherited a considerable amount of money, not to mention a 23-foot Gibbs of Hampton motor cruiser called *Serenade*. Built in 1947, and maintained regardless of cost, it provided his main recreation. The relative anonymity involved in river cruising was certainly in keeping with someone who ran an organisation which, in common with its Foreign Office partner, the Secret Intelligence Service (SIS), did not officially exist.

Boxted, his bespectacled Deputy Director, was ten years younger, though with his bald pate and slightly stooping stance, he had not aged particularly well. Like many of his colleagues, had come up from Cambridge with a First in languages – namely Russian, French and German. The tap on the shoulder came as he was about to cycle home after taking his finals. He was keen on astronomy, a subject which had captivated him since watching the BBC's 'Sky at Night' as a teenager. His partner, Kate, was also in the service – they had met during a mobile surveillance operation on a suspected IRA active service unit. The romance had had to wait, however. It was

54

well over a year before they could show their true feelings for each other, as the demands of working in the field were too great. They had no interest in getting married, and no desire for children. Kate loved cats and computers, interests which were not shared by Boxted to any great extent. When not looking through a telescope, he was in the garage tinkering with his VW Campervan, bought off the street on London's South Bank from a group of intrepid antipodeans who had driven it from Australia.

Boxted was the touchstone that Sir Stephen relied upon more than any other. He had been his deputy for nearly three years, and sometimes the way they communicated bordered on the telepathic. Their afternoon meetings were often punctuated by a glass of amontillado from Sir Stephen's well-stocked Edwardian drinks cabinet. His fine oak desk, like much of the furniture, had moved with the service down the decades.

'Did Berkowitz have anything for us?' asked Boxted. Sir Stephen had just returned from one of his irregular meetings with him, which usually involved a stroll through the Park.

'He wasn't quite as oblique as usual, which may or may not be significant. He corroborated a report about an impending arms shipment to the Provisionals from Gaddafi. Apparently it's going to be a big one, incorporating just about everything on their wish list. So that means a substantial number of AK-47s, not to mention much heavier weapons. He has an asset in Malta who'll provide the necessary details.'

'Some Irish eyes aren't going to be smiling when we intercept that little lot. I don't suppose he mentioned anything about Segev going to Liverpool?'

'Hardly. That's well outside his usual orbit.'

'About ten minutes ago we received a flash from Special Branch... Segev arrived there earlier today with a someone called Sophie Zoborski.'

'*Zoborski?* Now there's a name I'm not likely to forget.' He called his secretary on the intercom: 'Mary, go to the Register, please. Bring me everything we have under Zoborski.'

Within a few minutes there was a quiet knock at the door. She handed over a box file and then left the room. 'Quite an interesting fellow,' said Sir Stephen, leafing through the first folder. 'We could have potentially doubled him had it not been for the death of his wife. According to the autopsy she suffered a cervical fracture – a broken neck – after a suspected hit and run.'

'That was well before my time,' said Boxted.

'Let me see... his codename was 'Octave', and in the early Fifties he'd been sending back reports on the comings and goings at RAF Cullingthorpe in Leicestershire. It was one of several bases the Americans were upgrading for their strategic bombers. He confessed to being a Soviet agent well before the inquest, when he was interviewed by the police. The local superintendent – who had served with the Eighth Army in Italy – started asking questions about Octave's wartime service. The real Dominik Zoborski had been at Monte Cassino, and so had the superintendent... but not the man he was interviewing. Octave is actually Albert Grobinski, as German as any Prussian ever was. He even has an Iron Cross, First Class.'

'So was he the first of many "legends"?'

(For many years there was no possibility of using computer analysis of residential registration documents to uncover legends with false names and identities. When this technology became widely available in the 1960s, the Federal German BfV (domestic counterintelligence service), was able to net a significant number of East German agents who had supposedly 'resettled' in West Germany and West Berlin.)

'Indeed he was...' Sir Stephen was now poring over the contents of the second folder. 'We took him under our wing after he'd been picked up by Special Branch. He was granted immunity from prosecution on the understanding that he'd cooperate fully, which he most certainly did. There's an interesting note here about the reaction of the Polish government in exile, some of whom wanted him strung up in short order.'

'They must be the only government who meet in a restaurant.'

'Have you ever been to the Café Daquise?'

'I've never had the pleasure.'

'They've been meeting there since the war, practically. It's not exactly the House of Commons, though some might say that's no bad thing. I do recall sampling their beetroot soup – it was actually rather good. You ought to try it sometime.'

'I think I'll just take your word for it. Presumably we managed to placate them?'

'Indeed we did. After all, he was under our protection. I well remember the talk he gave to our course. You could have heard the proverbial pin drop. He told us his story and even coached us on how to send messages. We examined his code books, radio set and pistol – they were recovered from a cache in the woods near his home.'

'Funnily enough his daughter has a pistol as well – that's why she's been arrested.'

'We need to bring her in – Berkowitz also mentioned some kind of move being planned by the opposition. As you know, he's cultivated several good sources among the disaffected. One of them is dating a KGB officer with high-level access – and he talks in his sleep. According to Berkowitz, they have agents already in place over here that aren't attached to the embassy. That makes them more difficult to find, of course – yet for all we know they could be right under our noses.'

'The KGB could be blackmailing them, playing one against the other – "Do as we say or else". On the other hand, we could be wasting our time.'

'You need to see this addendum on Miss Zoborski, Adrian. She definitely merits further interest.'

Boxted summarised, reading out loud: 'Positively vetted when she joined the Intelligence Corps... posted British Army of the Rhine... nice photo of her in uniform... rather fetching, isn't she? Fluent in French and German, can translate Russian. Swam for the army. Oh, and according to this, she's also pretty handy with a pistol. If Octave's been reactivated, he'd be their mailbox – and she'd be a perfect fit for the fieldwork.'

'Could there be an overlap?'

'The file isn't flagged. Mind you, it would hardly be the first time they've held out on us.'

'Check for me, would you? We don't want to step on any delicate toes...'

57

They were referring to SIS, the occupants of Century House in Westminster Bridge Road, Lambeth. Uniformly bleak and utilitarian, this 22-storey tower block made MI5's HQ look like a Bauhaus masterpiece. Many thought it belonged more to the Moscow school of postwar architecture, the irony being the deep penetration of SIS by the KGB, which had continued from World War 2 up to the defection of double-agent Kim Philby in 1963 – barely a year before the building was completed.

Sir Stephen was back on the intercom: 'Another job for you, Mary. Contact operations at Northolt right away and ask them to position an aircraft at Liverpool – high priority.'

He turned back to Boxted: 'Who's available?'

'Gibson – I'm easing him back in after a spot of extended leave.'

'Ah yes...he's been in Belfast, hasn't he?'

'And done more than his fair share over there. He was overdue for a rest.'

'What's he doing now?'

'Helping out at Liverpool docks, screening ferry passengers from Ireland. I'm reluctant to put him back in the field just yet – not to any great extent, anyway. He's also been keeping an eye on those Russian cargo flights into West Midlands Airport.'

'I take it nothing startling has emerged?'

'According to his reports they've been as good as gold. They bring in cut price watches and cameras, and spares for those characterful cars of theirs – the ones favoured by our cash-strapped pensioners. Then they fly home with swag from the duty free shop – scotch, mostly. Christmas has come early for the comrades.'

'Let's re-assign him to look after Zoborski. We'd better start a fresh file on her. Oh, and track down her army records, would you? What artifice do you have in mind for her release?'

'Nothing too drastic. A slip of paper should do the trick.'

Boxted was soon on the line to MI5's regional office in Manchester. 'Drop everything, Gibbo – I've a nice little job for you back in Liverpool. You'll find a certain Sophie Zoborski at Speke police station. Don't leave there without her.'

'Russian?'

'English. My next call is to the local firearms department. They'll provide her with a firearms certificate, in the national interest.'

'Who's my contact?'

'A bod from Special Branch will smooth out any local difficulties. Take her straight to the airport. I'll meet you at Northolt.'

'Okay.'

'And by the way, Zoborski had a companion – Segev, one of Mossad's finest. He's probably back in London by now.'

Speke police station, 12.05pm

As Sophie entered the interview room, she had already resigned herself to a night in the cells. 'Looks like you could use a cup of tea,' said Keeley, following on behind.

'So could I,' said MacDonald.

'Ladies first,' she replied.

'I'd really appreciate that,' said Sophie, her spirits lifted somewhat by the Keeley's cheery disposition.

'How do you like it?' she asked.

'Strong… and two sugars, please.'

'I've got my own stash. The stuff that comes out of the machine tastes awful.' The kettle had nearly boiled when the phone rang: it was Chief Superintendent Matthews. 'Hello again, sir. This seems to be turning into the hotline.'

'It's hotter than you think. Where's your guv'nor?'

'He's about to interview Miss Zoborski. I'm making her a cuppa, actually.'

'Good girl, Karen. I want you to look after her.'

'She seems very nice...'

'She's also very important. Get him to call me as a matter of urgency.'

'Leave it with me, sir.'

She intercepted Copeland on his way to the interview room. He was scoffing a Mars bar. 'The Super wants you to call him right away.'

'Penny to a pound it's about Zaborinski.'

'That's right, guv – Miss Zoborski.'

'I was close enough.'

59

Keeley carried on making the tea as Copeland lifted the receiver and dialled...

'Thanks for calling back, Vince.'

'What's this all about?'

'Special Branch are coming for your prisoner.'

'And I'm just going to hand her over, is that it?'

'Look, this is big. She's going to walk whether we like it or not.'

'She's got a bloody gun, Dave!' Keeley winced as Copeland turned up the volume like a drill sergeant on a parade ground.

'For which she now has a firearms certificate, duly signed.'

'Since when?'

'Since now.'

'Suppose I drag my feet?'

'Don't force me to make a decision I might regret.'

'Aren't you forgetting something?'

'You're a good copper, Vince. But you know and I know that some of the villains you've banged up didn't do the jobs you arrested them for.'

'They still needed putting away.'

'Of course they did. But if you decide to be difficult, one or two of your old cases might have to be reopened'

'So it's blackmail?'

'I'm just pointing out the realities...'

'What about the realities at the golf club, eh? That chinless wonder friend of yours you went and recommended as treasurer?'

'Keep your voice down!'

Copeland had Matthews in his top pocket. It made him immune from any kind of threat – implied or otherwise. 'Some club treasurer he turned out to be – hands in the till from day one – and who sorted him out for you?'

'Please, Vince. Just do as I ask.'

They had started on the beat together, but Matthews was the one who knew how to pass the exams and progress up the greasy political pole. Copeland was the hard-nosed, no-nonsense grafter, the one who knew his way around the sleazy world of crime and criminals.

60

'Are you still there?' asked an anxious Matthews. Copeland was in no hurry to answer. The silence hung in the air like the smoke from his cigarette.

'Vince? Vince? For god's sake...'

'Okay, okay... keep your wig on. Just remember who your bloody friends are, that's all.'

'I'll see you get full recognition for this... for your cooperation.'

'I don't give a flying fuck about the recognition. Just get me some scotch – you know, the good stuff, the stuff your friends at the golf club drink.'

'I'll drop a case off at your place. Thanks again, Vince.'

'You know me, anything to be of service.'

Liverpool Airport, 2.22pm

A de Havilland DH.104 Devon, one of a dwindling number of RAF piston-engine communications aircraft, was parked on the edge of the apron, as far away as possible from the telephoto lenses pointed at it by a small group of plane spotters. When they boarded, Sophie and Gibson would not be in their direct line-of-sight or of anyone else who happened to be in the public viewing areas.

'That's unusual,' said one of the spotters.

'Haven't seen one of those here before,' replied his pal, busy writing its serial number in his notebook.

Gibson had taken charge of the Tokarev, stowing it away in the baggage compartment at the rear of the cabin. Sophie had never been in a Devon before – it was a type normally reserved for senior officers and VIPs. She relaxed in the large and comfortable seats and, looking ahead, could see the two pilots at work in the cockpit. Puffs of exhaust smoke shot back under the wing as the first of its two Gipsy Queen engines burst into life.

'Time to buckle in,' said Gibson.

The aircraft climbed away and turned south-east. When they reached their cruising altitude at 7,500 feet, the engines were throttled back and the cabin became noticeably quieter. Gibson seemed friendly enough, though they'd hardly spoken on the journey to the airport. She reckoned he was about the same age as Segev, though the darkness under his eyes made him look older. He had a

61

shock of dark wavy hair that he swept back with his hand from time to time.

'When did you last eat anything?' he asked.

'Nothing much since breakfast.'

He went to a locker near the cabin door and came back with a large flask, two mugs and two robust brown paper bags containing a selection of sandwiches, crisps, chocolate bars and fruit.

'How do you like your coffee? NATO standard?'

'I prefer it black, please.'

'Help yourself to a sandwich. The roast beef and tomato looks okay – or there's ham and cheese...'

She was quite hungry, and decided to have one of each. She was also hungry for information. 'So you work for the Home Office?'

'That's right.'

'Which department, exactly?'

'Let's just say I specialise in security, shall we?'

She knew that meant MI5, but decided not to mention it. 'I think Segev does, too. We came up by helicopter this morning... it's not often I fly twice in one day. I guess this is fairly serious?'

'Trust me – anything that involves someone like Segev is serious.'

'Oh, I didn't realise...'

'You can tell us all about it when we get to Northolt.'

'There's not much to tell... he wasn't exactly effusive.'

'I'll look that up in the dictionary when I get home.' His face broke into a smile. She smiled back.

'When we land at Northolt we're going to have a chat about what happened today.'

'We could do that now, couldn't we?'

'We could, but you'd only have to repeat everything to my boss.'

Another day, another boss, she thought.

'I hear you work for an advertising agency?'

'I'm supposed to be working up a new account. Now I'm beginning to wish I'd stayed in the army.'

'I'm ex-forces, too... including five years in the Legion.'

'You mean the French Foreign Legion?'

'Yep.'

62

'That's amazing! But how –'

'Did I end up doing this? We were trained to do everything, and I became a communications specialist. That stood me in good stead for what came later. Not that I can say much about it.'

'That's a coincidence – I started out as a radio telegraphist, then graduated to intelligence and security work. Not that I can say much about it.'

Gibson grinned. 'Touché.'

'Life in the Legion can be pretty rough, can't it?'

'It can – especially if you're a Brit. I'd been a Marine – that is until I rashly decided it wasn't exciting enough. The beastings were on a whole new level until one of the frogs felt sorry for me. He told me to learn German. It was good advice. Most of the officers were German – though not, as some people seem to think, from the Waffen SS. By the end of my initial training I knew enough to get by, and I never had any trouble after that.'

The steady beat of the engines changed as the aircraft began a gradual descent towards RAF Northolt. Gibson went forward to confer with the pilots. He came back with the news that they would be landing in ten minutes.

In contrast, Segev would soon be departing from Heathrow, but this time the destination would be Madrid. There was no point in trying to explain away what had gone wrong to a man like Berkowitz. His response was blunt: 'Not like you to screw up, my friend.'

'How could I have known she had a Tokarev?'

'Forget it. It's time we took care of Arnold.'

'I've thought of something that won't alert the Spanish to our presence – a honey trap. His taste for hookers is well known, and he likes to experiment. We'll fix him with auto erotic asphyxiation. The sexual kick should be irresistible – and lethal. The girl will use a scarf to take him to the point of unconsciousness. And then, instead of releasing the ligature…'

'That's what I like about you, my friend – you're so imaginative.'

'It will look like an accident. It's too bad about Zoborski – he was into her, no question.'

'Who else do you have in mind?'

'Rachel. She's a real tigress. We used her in Beirut last year. Arnold's notoriously picky, but she's definitely his type. She'll have to pander to him, yet retain control. He's a lot smarter than he looks.'

'Cover?'

'Dancer waiting for one of the cruise ships that come into Malaga – he'll go for that, for sure. She can pick him up from his favourite bar in the town. He likes to lie in wait drinking vodka martinis, pretending to be James Bond, eyeing up the kusit.'

Meanwhile, Sophie was being introduced to Boxted in the VIP lounge at RAF Northolt: 'I'm very pleased to meet you, Miss Zoborski.'

'Thank you. I'm still trying to come to terms with all this, if I'm honest.'

'Please take a seat. May I call you Sophie?'

'Of course.'

She sat in the middle of a semicircle of armchairs, Boxted taking the one on her left. This was now familiar territory. 'Before we go any further,' said Boxted, 'is there anything you'd like to tell me?'

'What do you mean?'

'Who you might be working for, for instance?'

'I work for SJ Advertising – at least, that's what I've been trying to do.'

'The reason I ask is that you have a most impressive CV, one that might attract the attention of another intelligence service.'

'I'm flattered. As a matter of fact I did think about it, but how do you apply? I never went to Oxbridge, so I thought my chances would be pretty slim anyway.'

'We now live in more enlightened times, Sophie. Things are beginning to change.'

'I'm glad to hear it.'

'It's time we had a little talk about what's happened over the past few days. I have to make it clear that this interview, and any subsequent dealings you may have with us, are covered by the Official Secrets Act. Now, tell me about Segev... how did you get mixed up with him?'

'We met in the pool at Crystal Palace.'

'By arrangement?'

'Hardly. I'd never seen him before.'

'What did you talk about?'

'Nothing much. Not at the beginning, anyway.'

'But you hit it off with him, just like that?'

'I'd just broken up with my boyfriend. I guess he caught me on the rebound.'

'Apart from the obvious – you're rather pretty – why did Segev want to meet you?'

'He was very interested in Tony Arnold. I was introduced to him by my boss, Sandy Johnson. He's directed a lot of commercials for Sandy.'

'Segev seems to think Arnold's doing a lot more than that.'

'He could be right – you should see Arnold's collection of weapons. But it's all World War 2 stuff, nothing modern – if that means anything. I can tell you he's no friend of Israel. Apparently his dad was murdered by the Stern Gang.'

'I see... and your job involves working with Arnold, presumably?'

'That was the general idea. I ended up being alone with him in his house. Sandy should have been there as well, but he had to stay behind. The plan was to meet up, then go out for a working lunch.'

'What happened?'

'Arnold went for me. He fancies himself like – I'd rather not use the word – and I was in serious trouble until Sandy managed to phone him. That gave me enough time to get out of there.'

'When did you meet Segev again?'

'Shortly afterwards... I decided to stop in the village for a cuppa – and to call Sandy.'

'And Segev followed you, I take it?'

'I think he was watching the house.'

'How come you ended up in Liverpool?'

'It was after I'd met his boss, some guy called Abel –'

'Berkowitz. He's head of station for Israeli intelligence in London.'

'Apart from insisting that Dad had a false identity, he said I'd got an aunt called Drusilla Williams. I had to get to the truth, and Segev took me to visit her – that's why I was in Liverpool. It seems she really is my aunt. She showed me some old photos, including one of an American serviceman called Todd.'

'That would be Lieutenant Todd Casey, United States Air Force. I've delved into the files concerning your mother's death, including the evidence given at the inquest. Casey gave a full statement to the police. He gave her a lift part of the way home, and it appears that after he dropped her off something went terribly wrong. He was probably the last person to see her alive.'

'Why didn't he appear at the inquest?'

'He flew back to America the day before it opened. We'll probably never know precisely what happened. Casey was in the clear – there was no suspicion of foul play. Even if there had been, he was beyond our jurisdiction – the extradition arrangements we have with America only go one-way.'

'I see...'

'Getting back to Segev, as we must, your arrest may have been a blessing in disguise.'

'He's been linked with what the CIA call wet jobs – assassinations,' said Gibson. 'After what happened at the airport, he'll probably lie low for a while. He might even be on his way back to Tel Aviv.'

'We arranged to meet at my flat this evening.'

'I doubt he'll turn up,' said Boxted, 'but now would be a good time to give us your new address.'

Gibson reached for his notebook. 'Write it down here... and add your telephone number.'

'You'll find I'm ex-directory.'

They left RAF Northolt in the kind of black London taxi that doesn't pick up fares. Boxted hadn't switched off: 'I suppose you picked up your flair for languages from your father?'

'He still has an accent, though he's always been well spoken. He certainly has a good command of English.'

'That's more than most English people have these days,' said Gibson.

'That's a bit awkward,' she said. 'My new company car is still at Fairoaks. I only picked it up yesterday.'

66

Gibson smiled. 'At least you didn't leave it at Heathrow. The cost goes through the roof if you overstay.'

'I'd like Gary to pay your visit father a visit. Do you think tomorrow would be alright?'

'Why do you – ?'

'I think it might be important. Perhaps you'd like to go with him? He can take you there in one of our cars.'

'That's fine by me. I've been given some time off, and I need to see Dad anyway.'

It took just over an hour to reach her flat. 'I'll pick you up tomorrow at ten,' said Gibson, 'I prefer to miss the morning rush.'

She was tired, but resisted the urge to flop straight onto the settee. Instead she ran a bubble bath, swirling the water to create a deep, fragrant cloud. Soon she was half-asleep in her sea of tranquillity. The tranquillity didn't last long – someone was knocking at her front door. The knocking became louder and more persistent. Her eyes flicked open. *I hope that isn't Giles,* she thought. *I really don't need this right now.* She grabbed a towel, stabbed her feet into a pair of flip-flops, and set off towards the front door.

'Is that you, Giles?'

'Hurry up gorgeous... the champers is getting warm.' It wasn't Giles. It wasn't Segev. It was the last person on earth she wanted to see. It was Tony Arnold. She spoke with conviction: 'Please leave. I'm not going to let you in… not now, not ever.'

'Now don't be like that, baby. I just want to make it up to you, that's all.'

She saw the door handle move up and down. It was like a scene from a third-rate horror movie. That's when she realised she hadn't locked the door completely. Arnold applied all his weight to it, but the Yale lock held – just. She rushed forward to ram home the bolt and fix the chain. Being shut out displeased him more than somewhat. 'I've tried to be nice to you…'

To her great relief the next voice she heard was Gibson's: 'Lost your key, old son?'

'Who the hell are you?'

'Let's just say I'm a friend, shall we?'

67

Sophie was listening at the door. 'Tell him to go away and leave me alone.'

'I think the lady's made her feelings perfectly clear, don't you?' said Gibson.

'I just want to apologize for what –'

'Of course you do, matey. Bravo. Now do as the lady asks.'

Arnold sensed – correctly – that if he didn't go, Gibson was prepared to use more than words.

'Here, make sure she gets this.' He gave Gibson the champagne, then went back to his BMW. There was a chirrup from his rear tyres as he floored the accelerator. After a few seconds, brake lights blazing, he darted down a side street.

'And goodnight to you, too,' said Gibson.

She opened the door slowly at first, just to make sure Arnold had gone. 'You'd better come in...' She closed the door – and bolted it.

'Who was that charm school graduate?'

'That was Tony Arnold – he's certainly got some nerve. I thought you weren't coming back until tomorrow?'

'We thought there was a slim chance Segev might turn up. Arnold didn't come empty-handed – Bollinger, Nineteen Seventy-Six. He's certainly no cheapskate, I'll give him that.'

'He's got money alright – I've seen some of his invoices. That doesn't cut any ice with me.'

Gibson pointed at the champagne. 'Where shall I – ?'

'I think you'll find there's plenty of room in the fridge. I haven't had time to do much shopping.'

'By the way, you've got a bit of soap under your chin.'

She wiped it away with her fingers. 'I'd better put something on.' Their eye contact was more than fleeting.

'Yes... don't catch cold.'

'You sound like my Dad.'

Gibson smiled. It was difficult to believe she could be involved in anything darker than her day job. Difficult, but not impossible. After a few minutes she re-entered the living room, brushing her hair briskly. She was wearing a powder blue silk dressing gown. The hem was about four inches above knee level. He'd already admired her bare, tanned shoulders, and her legs did not disappoint. He could hardly keep his eyes off them.

She stopped brushing for a moment. 'Can I get you anything? A coffee, perhaps?'

It took quite a lot of mental fortitude for him to give the appropriate answer in the circumstances. 'I'd better be on my way, actually. I'll see you in the morning.'

Not long after he'd left, the phone rang. She knew who it was: 'Hello, Dad.'

'I had to make sure you got home okay.'

'I'm just a little tired, that's all. I don't think I'll have much trouble sleeping tonight.'

'We must have a talk. There are things I need to tell you about Drusilla, about what happened after Elizabeth died.'

'Don't worry about it, Dad. I'm coming up to see you tomorrow, there's no –'

'I only wanted to protect you.'

'I know that. I understand.'

'You're coming up tomorrow, did you say?'

'We should be with you by midday.'

'We...?'

'I'll be arriving with a chap called Gary Gibson. He brought me back from Liverpool. He works for the Home Office.'

'I see... I'd better go in early and take the rest of the day off.'

'I doubt we'll be there for very long...'

'Safe journey, then. Love you.'

'Goodnight, Dad. Love you, too.'

Their conversation was recorded. Permission for a phone tap had been granted by a high court judge, as per normal procedure.

Wednesday, 22nd June, 8.33am

Sir Stephen and Boxted were listening to the playback.

'Any thoughts, Adrian?'

'Perfectly innocuous... nothing that sounded like a code word.'

'We must have certainty, Adrian. If she's sandbagging us, Gibson's probably in the best position to find out.'

Sophie had time to nip out for a pint of milk before Gibson arrived. On her way back she ran into a jolly pensioner who was walking his Jack Russell terrier. 'What on earth was all that about, darlin?'

'Sorry?'

'There was a bit of a barney outside your front door last night.'

'Oh yes – sorry about that. I hope it didn't disturb you...'

'After thirty years in the Merchant Navy it takes a lot to disturb me, darlin. Mark Hutchinson's me name – everyone calls me "Hutch". I'm in the flat a few doors along with the old boiler, otherwise known as me wife, Flo.'

'You're both retired now...?'

'We're living the dream, darlin. It's our pearl wedding anniversary next week.'

'Congratulations! I'm Sophie by the way...'

'Pleased to meet you, I'm sure,' he said, giving her a firm handshake. 'Who was that other bloke?'

'That was Gary. He's coming round again this morning.'

'Your fella is he?'

'Not exactly. Just someone I'm working with at the moment.'

'Sorry, darlin – mustn't stick me nose in.'

'That's alright. He's a nice guy, actually.'

'He had a mate with him. You know, from the council.'

'The council?'

'He was in a van parked round the corner. I wouldn't have seen him, except Boozer – that's me dog – hadn't done his business the first time, so we goes round the block. That's when I saw him having a quiet word.'

'It's certainly been nice meeting you, Hutch. Thanks for looking out for me.'

'The pleasure's all mine, darlin. Look after yourself.'

Back in the flat, she rang the office. 'Hi, Georgie. Just thought I'd check in...'

'How are you?'

'Guess who had an unexpected visitor last night? Tony Arnold made a personal appearance.'

'Oh no! You're alright, aren't you...?'

'I had a bodyguard – and he rescued a bottle of champagne as well.'

'No! When did you meet him?'

'It's not like that, exactly…'

'Don't hold out on me, Sophie. Who is he?'

'Just someone who happened along...'

'Are you seeing him again?'

'In about half an hour.'

'How exciting!'

'We're going up to Leicester. It's strictly business, okay?'

'I'll see you when I see you. Oh, Sandy says I can pick up your Saab from Fairoaks. And I thought you'd like to know our favourite sleazebag flew out to Spain first thing.'

'I think that deserves a champagne celebration.'

'Definitely! Safe journey – don't do anything I wouldn't do!'

Chapter V

In Moscow, it was time to break the news of Operation VIKTOR. The moment the briefing room door swung open, his crew jumped to attention. Koslov had the kind of charisma that preceded him like a bow wave. They admired him greatly, both as a pilot of rare ability and as a tactician par excellence.

He addressed them from the podium. 'Sit down you old reprobates. Our next visit to England is going to be far from routine. We've been chosen for a special mission. Our job is to collect a package from under the noses of the British. The importance of this mission cannot be overstated. Effective from midday on Thursday, you'll be confined to base until our positioning flight to East Berlin. Absolute security is essential.

'As you know, for the past few months we've been alternating with Major Ostapenko's crew on the fortnightly cargo run to West Midlands Airport. This time it's going to be different, which is why this afternoon we'll be having some refresher training on tactical landings and take-offs. We need to make sure we can land, load and leave in record time. I can't tell you any more at this stage, though there's a good chance you'll have a little more to spend in the duty free shop. Just remember that any items you purchase are for you and your immediate family only. I don't want any black marketeers.'

'You may be too late.' said Shushkin.

Koslov always enjoyed the banter among his crew, and he was a willing contributor.

'Your rank will not protect you, Major.'

Shushkin smiled. 'It's our flight engineer who needs protecting. Isn't that right, Sitev? Tell the Colonel about the blonde behind the foreign exchange desk.'

Koslov spared his blushes. 'Stick to jeans and whisky, they'll give you a lot less trouble.'

The only person who didn't laugh was the political officer tasked with communicating the Party's perspective on just about everything from international affairs to binge drinking. Somewhat chubby, and with a personality as colourless as his face, Captain Oleg Malenkovich knew he wasn't exactly popular. His presence was tolerated with a kind of detached resignation. After adding a few more lines in his notebook he spoke up: 'With your permission, Colonel, I would like to make a short statement.'

'Go ahead, comrade.'

'First of all, let me say that I have every confidence in you and your men. However, may I remind you all not to jump to false conclusions during your next visit to what is, after all, a capitalist state. Don't be deceived by the veneer of prosperity on display at the airport. England is riven by high unemployment and the drugs and crime that go with it. A decadent and privileged elite own most of the land and property. The workers are kept down by the constant fear of unemployment. They know little of the equality we take for granted here in the Motherland. They listen to music that is degenerate, they read –'

'That's enough for now, comrade,' said Koslov. 'We're on a tight schedule.'

M1 northbound, 10.42am

Gibson joined the motorway and accelerated his Vauxhall Carlton smoothly up to 70 miles per hour. Sophie was wearing her favourite blue jeans, matching denim jacket and a white tee shirt. She flicked back her hair, then adjusted her new aviator sunglasses.

'You're quiet,' she said. 'Penny for your thoughts.'

'I wish I was a mind reader.'

She laughed. And that made him smile. He hadn't felt this good in a very long time. Yet he felt like an intruder, digging ever more deeply into a life she had every right to keep private. His mind was still stacking up the ifs, buts and maybes when her soft voice broke through: 'Are you listening to me, Gary?'

'Hanging on your every word.'

'I asked you about your women.'

'Women?'

'You know, people like me. The opposite sex.'

'There isn't much to tell…'

She glanced across at him, raising her eyebrows slightly: 'Now come on, Gary. I bet you had a girl in every fort.'

'I was hardly Britain's answer to Beau Geste...'

'Are sure about that? I can picture you riding a camel...'

They started to laugh. She stopped first, only to restart when he gave her a crossed-eyed, quizzical look.

'You're funny,' she said.

'*I'm* funny?'

'Don't set me off again. Just give.'

He moved his hand from forehead to chin in a karate chop. 'Serious face.'

'I'm waiting Gary...'

'I was based in Corsica most of time, *not* the Sahara. I met Jazz in Paris on my first leave. She was working as a waitress –'

'In a cocktail bar?'

'No, in a bistro near the opera house. Do you want to know or not?'

'Sorry, Gary. Go on...'

'I sat down, ordered steak and chips and a glass of beer. I didn't pay much attention to her at first.'

'With a name like that she ought to be interesting.'

'That was my pet name for her. She was called Nathalie... Nathalie Jasserand.'

'Tell me about your mademoiselle,' she said, lowering her voice.

'She was a madame, actually.'

'Je pensais que tu étais un peu un cheval sombre...'

'She wanted a divorce, if that makes it any better.'

'Did she get one? The divorce, I mean.'

'Unfortunately not. They were Roman Catholics and, if that wasn't enough, her old man, Eric, said she'd end up with nothing if she ever went through with it. We'd tried to be discreet. All my letters and postcards went to her sister, Véronique. We first met about a year before I came out, and after that I saw her as often as I could. Eric played cards – for money. Jazz would phone me as soon as he'd left for the big game, which was usually every Saturday night. He wouldn't get back until four or five o'clock the next morning. That gave us time to go out if we wanted to, which is what we'd decided to do the day he came back early.

'He saw us getting into a taxi. Jazz called me on the Monday. She was crying, poor kid. I went over there – it was dull, overcast, and the streets were like lead. She was waiting outside, wearing sunglasses. That's when she told me it was over. I thought about going in and sorting him out, but I bottled it. So I kissed her for the last time, then walked away. So that was that, la fin de l'affaire.'

'Sounds like the plot of a Francois Truffaut movie.'

'At least it wasn't a total waste – she taught me how to make a good omelette.'

'Is that all?'

'Possibly a few other things...'

'What did she look like?'

'Brunette, quite tall, ace face. She didn't need much makeup.'

'Brown eyes?'

'What do you want me to say? That she looked a bit like you?'

'Just trying to make conversation. We're nearly there now, anyway.'

Her father lived in a council maisonette, the same one that he and Sophie had moved into in the early 1960s. The door was unlocked, and they walked straight in. The hug he gave her said everything. 'Let me up for air, Dad!'

He released her, then shook hands with Gibson. 'Thank you for coming.'

'I've been looking forward to meeting you.'

'Come through and sit down. Are you going to put the kettle on, Sophie?'

'In a minute. Here's your present.'

He unwrapped it carefully, revealing volume one of Chopin's Nocturnes, an RCA recording by Arthur Rubinstein. 'You shouldn't have Sophie – but thank you.' They hugged again.

'Dad's a big fan of Rubinstein.'

'He can play Chopin better than anyone. No one can match him.'

'I'm ashamed to say I know very little about classical music,' said Gibson. 'I wouldn't know a nocturne from a nutcracker.'

'Dad's got an amazing collection. He's a supporter of the LSO.'

'That was all Sophie's idea. I only found out when I received the literature through the post. She certainly looks after me, that daughter of mine.'

While Sophie went to make the tea, Gibson took in the room. There was a cabinet full of medals and trophies, all won in swimming competitions. There were school photos on the sideboard and on the mantelpiece above the gas fire. Also on the mantelpiece was a single, Madonna-like photo of Elizabeth holding Sophie in her arms.

She came through with a large tray, laden with a full tea service and a plate full of chocolate digestives. 'These are Dad's favourite.'

'Let me take that,' said Gibson.

'It's okay – I can manage.' She placed the tray on the coffee table.

'I seem to remember you'd go through half a packet of those in no time when you were in training. And if I turned my back for five minutes the fridge would be empty.'

She smiled. 'I needed the calories.'

They sipped their tea and ate their biscuits until the small talk dried up. There was then a pregnant pause before she and Gibson began to hear her father's story.

'Yes, I am Albert Grobinski. I was brought up in Breslau, Poland. We were Germans first and Poles second – though we all hated the Russians. When I was called up in April of Forty-Three, I saw it as my duty to fight – everyone did.

'I went straight into the infantry. There was already a shortage. I was lucky in that my father, Karl, knew about radios – knowledge that he passed on to me. He was a watch repairer by trade, but had branched out into supplying radios. He had a small shop, and when I was old enough I used to go in and help him out on Saturday mornings.

'I did three months basic training, then some specialist training as a radioman. Most of the men – boys really – went straight to the Eastern Front, but I was posted to a barracks near Antwerp, Belgium. As postings go it was one of the better ones. We were about as safe as we could be in wartime. The resistance groups were shadowy, and far away. We were a garrison army, with plenty of time on our hands.

'One night I was nursing a drink in one of the local dives when another soldier came in, as drunk as a lord. He was a radioman, too, and told me that one of his English-speaking friends had been posted to a special unit in The Hague.'

'Careless talk,' said Gibson.

'Lucky no one was eavesdropping. I put a finger to my lips, and he took the hint. We feared only two things – the Gestapo and the local prostitutes.'

'What happened then?' asked Gibson. He and Sophie smiled at each other.

'I went to see my commanding officer, and he said he'd make enquiries on my behalf. I began to study English whenever I could, as I knew there would be some kind of test. It gave me something to do, a goal to aim for.

'My luck ran out when my turn came for guard duty. One night a visiting Oberst – major – drove up to the gate with a beauty in the passenger seat. I checked their papers, and she gave me the most wonderful smile. The next evening I met her again – quite by chance – in a local cafe. Her name was Catherine, and, even though I knew she was forbidden fruit, I asked to sit down. And we started talking. That's when Herr Oberst reappeared. He fixed me alright, said I'd volunteered for the Eastern Front. At least it looked good on my record, and I got a few days extra leave into the bargain. That was the last time I saw Breslau looking anything like her pre-war best. The city was still untouched – at least physically. After Antwerp, the food was awful... and it was going to get a lot worse.'

'Did you – or your parents – have any sense of how badly the war was going?' asked Gibson.

'They desperately wanted to believe the propaganda that said no Russian soldier would ever set foot on German soil. We were told the Red Army would be stopped in its tracks, that our defences would be too strong for them. I also held out such hopes – until I arrived in Ukraine. I joined the reconstituted 6th Army – the one we lost at Stalingrad. At first we managed to hold the line. Then all hell broke loose. We fell back, regrouped, even counter-attacked... but always weaker than before. New units were being scraped together... what few reserves we had were asked to perform miracles. The Ivans just got stronger and stronger. They crossed the river Dnieper and took Kiev, then pushed us back across the Polish border. What we went through… I still have nightmares, even now...

'I was older than most of them. Some were barely out of short trousers. In the final months we had to fight without any air cover or tank support. We dug in behind a minefield... and waited. We began to hear their artillery. It sounded like distant thunder, and at night the whole skyline would light up. A few optimists in out battalion thought the artillery might be ours, as we had none firing from our rear in reply. That was until the first shells began to fall on our positions.

'Historians talk about the Soviet steamroller. Well, I saw it. We gave a good account of ourselves with mortars, machine-guns and panzerfaust. But they just kept coming. They were unstoppable. Eventually their tanks and infantry came straight through us. My best friend, Klaus, shot the man who was about to stick me. Shooting at the enemy is one thing, but when you're fighting hand-to-hand it's savagery, no more. By now we weren't fighting for the Fatherland anymore. We were fighting for each other, for survival.

'As night fell Klaus and I managed to scramble away and hide in some woods nearby. As far as we could tell we were the only ones left. We'd taken all the water and food we could carry from the Russians lying in and around our trench, including tins of spam. From America! We could hardly believe it.

'In the woods our ears became attuned to the slightest sound. We'd stop every ten or twenty minutes, just to listen. The thing we feared most was stumbling into the path of some partisans or the special military police. Either way we'd already decided to go down fighting, because there would be no point in surrendering.

'Each night we bedded down as best we could. We had ground sheets, and slept under our greatcoats. The nights were terribly cold – that's when you find out what being chilled to the bone really means. How I would dream about lying in a warm bed! After weeks of living rough we were filthy, hungry and desperately tired. So when we emerged next to what looked like a main road, we flopped just inside the tree line to take stock. I could hardly think straight, but Klaus could still read a map. He'd been a forester before the war.'

'Where were you?' asked Gibson.

'About ten kilometres west of Posnań. There was no point in trying to get home – we'd been thrown back hundreds of kilometres. We feared for our families. I kept reading the last letter my mother, Maria, had sent me. She told me to be brave, that they were waiting to be evacuated. They'd be going without my father – he'd been arrested by the Gestapo and sentenced to death by a people's court.'

'But why, Dad?'

'Wehrkraftzersetzung – undermining the German war effort. Apparently he'd been overheard saying that the situation was hopeless, and that the Nazis were blaming everyone but themselves. Ethnic Germans were ordered to stay put, and by the time they were allowed to evacuate there was little or no transport available – they had to leave virtually everything behind. I knew in my heart of hearts that I'd never see my parents, or my younger sister, Gisela, ever again. Everything I'd known or cared for was falling apart.'

'I wish you'd told me all this before.'

'I wanted to wait until you were older, but I never seemed to find the right moment. I'm trying to make up for it now.'

'There's nothing to make up for, Dad.'

'We ended up in the Courland Pocket. After the surrender we feared the worst, and were reluctant to come out into the open. We'd seen so many bodies by the roadside or in ditches – the smell was appalling. And not all of them were soldiers by any means. Klaus and I threw away our weapons and started to walk down this road... and the first vehicle that came along was an American truck, a Studebaker. Our joy didn't last very long. It was full of Russians.'

'Lend-lease,' said Gibson. 'From Uncle Sam to Uncle Joe.'

'How could we win? It was impossible.'

'Yet you fought on,' said Gibson. 'How did they treat you?'

'The ones in the truck must have been from a crack Guards regiment. Their officer spoke good German. The first thing they did was open up our jackets and shirts. If they'd found an SS tattoo we'd have been shot on the spot. They searched us pretty roughly, but didn't hit us or anything. The brutality came later... from other troops.

'We were taken to some sort of holding camp. The officer spoke to someone – I assumed it was the commandant – and they took down our details. We were nearly mad with hunger, but they gave us nothing to eat. We slept in huts that weren't fit for pigs. We had no bedding, no blankets. There was no point in complaining – unless you wanted to dig your own grave. Klaus and I spent the days trying not to catch the eye of any of the guards.

'We knew that prisoners were being forced to sign confessions for supposed crimes against the Russians. Those who resisted were shown no mercy. I'd already decided to sign whatever they wanted me to sign – if I lived that long.

'One morning I was put in front of two NKVD officers. They'd seen the signaller flashes on my uniform. They asked me if I spoke English. I said yes. I found it easy to lie about radio intercept work against the British. I was given a simple choice: work for them or march to Russia with the others. So I had a new identity – Zoborski's. They told me he'd been "liquidated" for refusing to cooperate. So I cooperated.'

'You did what you had to do,' said Gibson. 'Not many lived to see Germany again.'

'How many Russian PoWs had we starved to death? They were paying us back in kind. Even if I'd managed to escape, there was no home to go back to anyway. Later on I learned how the Poles had taken their revenge, even against innocent civilians. Those that weren't expelled or murdered right away were sent to concentration camps – the same ones the Nazis had used. And there were plenty of Russians who needed no excuse to join in the killing.

'Once I'd agreed to help, one of them made me hand over the last family photo I had... and burnt it before my eyes. After that, they gave me some potato soup and a few slices of bread – the first meal I'd had for nearly a fortnight – and told me I'd be sent to Moscow for training and "political re-education". When I asked after Klaus, they said he'd have to take his chances with the others. There was nothing I could do to help him. Before they took me out of the camp they gave me some soap, a razor and some clean clothes. Whatever doubts I had were dispelled by the instinct to survive.

'The journey to Moscow seemed to take forever. The trains were slow, and I was glad to catch up on some sleep. Being guarded by the NKVD had its advantages. I ate what they ate, and that included more spam... and tushonka.'

Gibson raised his eyebrows. 'Tushonka?'

'Tinned pork with lard, onions and spices – another gift from the Americans.'

'By the way, Dad's never lost his taste for spam.'

'I like it fried – with chips and beans it makes a good meal.'

Gibson nodded. 'I'll second that. So what happened to you in Moscow?'

'Political indoctrination... day in, day out. Western imperialism was the new enemy. The socialist revolution had to be defended. Britain and America were denounced again and again. I kept thinking: Why are they turning against the very people who had helped to crush the Nazis? It didn't seem to make any sense.'

'It did to Stalin,' said Gibson. 'And no one, but no one dared to challenge his distrust of the Western allies. The fact that we were already demobilising on a grand scale didn't seem to make any difference.'

'Politics is one thing, but what really mattered to me was that my health was getting better all the time, and I certainly enjoyed improving my English. Some of the agent craft – such as encoding messages – was just an extension of what I'd learned as a signaller. I was gradually coming to terms with my new existence, though it was impossible not to keep thinking about what had happened to my family. But I had to keep my feelings under the surface. I was determined to tow the line, to be a model student. When they said I was going to England – well, it just seemed incredible.

'They gave me a ticket for a passage to Liverpool by tramp steamer, the *Anna Carlson*. It had a big Swedish flag painted on the side. The voyage from Stettin took well over a week. My cabin was small but comfortable. The food was wholesome. I remember the pickled herrings, freshly baked bread and real coffee. I felt guilty and enormously uplifted at the same time. I enjoyed being at sea. I was

81

even thinking about signing on as a deckhand and disappearing off to South America. But then I remembered what one of my minders had said to me before I walked up the gangplank: "If you ever betray us, we do not forgive – or forget."

'The night we entered the North Sea a storm was brewing. I couldn't sleep – whenever a big wave hit the side of the ship it sounded like an artillery barrage. While we were waiting to dock, I came out on deck for my first view of Liverpool. The wind had dropped, and I remember feeling the warmth of the sun on my face – a good omen, I thought. There were ships everywhere, great walls of grey and black as far as you could see. The buildings were the same – those that were left anyway.'

'I think it was the most heavily bombed city after London,' said Gibson. 'Had it been destroyed the convoys that carried the troops and supplies from America would have had to go somewhere else. It also played a key role in defeating the U-boats in the Atlantic... so what happened when you disembarked?'

'I expected to spend hours explaining myself to customs and immigration, but it was all over in a matter of minutes. They stamped my papers, then gave me directions for the Seaman's Mission. I was just about to walk inside when I saw this young woman walking towards me. I can see her now... she was wearing a green dress with white polka dots... her hair was full and flowing. I was spellbound... she was just so beautiful. See looked at me, but carried on down the street – I never thought I'd see her again.

'The next day I was killing time in the British Restaurant round the corner. It was busy... I could hardly believe my luck when the same girl came in and sat down opposite me. That's how I met Liz.'

'After all you'd been through,' said Sophie, 'something good came along.'

We just clicked right from the start. She told me she'd just lost her factory job and wasn't all that happy at home. I told her I'd be at the Seaman's Mission, but would have to leave soon. We saw each other nearly every day for a week, and by then we were in love – she wanted to come with me to Leicester. That didn't go down too well with her parents, or her younger sister, Drusilla. "You'd be living in sin," they said. But Liz had made up her mind: "We could get married." So we eloped. We were both very lapsed Catholics, so we decided to tie the knot at Leicester registry office.

'There was no time or money for a honeymoon. We registered for our ration books, then hopped on a tram to the employment office. I was still self-conscious about my accent and feared my papers wouldn't stand much scrutiny. So I didn't argue when I was sent to a building site in Braunstone. I started at the bottom, as a general labourer digging foundations for prefabs. At least I now had a national insurance number, and being married to Liz meant that my "naturalisation" – as it was called – didn't really need much help from the Polish Resettlement Corps. Fate was being kind to me.

'Liz charmed everyone she met – including the man at the employment office. She was sent to Richardson's Chemists, right in the city centre. She worked at the counter, and also helped him to make up the prescriptions. Old Richardson could hardly believe his luck – I think the number of prescriptions doubled within a week.

'Our biggest headache was finding somewhere to live. A prefab would've been ideal, but we were too far down the list. Then Liz helped again. One of her customers was a retired schoolmistress, and she had a small bungalow on the outskirts of town. She wanted someone to look after the property while she went over to Ireland to care for her elder sister. Liz explained our situation and she agreed to let the property to us until she needed to return. We stayed there until late Nineteen Forty-Eight. By then Liz was expecting, and we qualified for a prefab. They were good little houses – warm, all mod cons, and the neighbours were as house proud as we were. We had peace and quiet and security.'

'What was she like as a baby?' asked Gibson.

'Nothing but trouble.' Sophie laughed. 'We brought her back on the bus from the hospital. Liz had this glow about her. Sophie was wrapped up so tight you could hardly see her face. After we put her in the crib we hugged each other out of sheer joy. It was a special time... a very happy time.'

'So outwardly you were just a young couple making a home – a life – for yourselves. But in the background...'

'Yes... that was always preying on my mind. I had to be careful.'

'You were being paid, of course? I mean, in addition to your normal work?'

'It would come in a mixture of one pound and ten shilling notes from a dead drop at Leicester station. If there was anything for me there'd be a chalk mark on one of the stanchions. A package would be tucked under the eleventh stair from the bottom on the down platform – a convenient height for a fairly unobtrusive retrieval.

'I needed to be more mobile and somewhere to hide my radio set. Buying a car was out of the question, so I picked up a war surplus BSA M20 and fitted a sidecar. Liz wouldn't travel in it with Sophie, and when I needed to get on the key there were several secluded places I could use.'

'Where did the set come from?' asked Gibson.

'It was a suitcase radio – a British Type A Mk III – and completely self-contained. The Russians didn't waste anything. A ticket arrived in the post and I collected it from the left luggage office at the station.'

'You'd managed to move on from labouring at this stage?' Gibson had never heard a story like this before, at first-hand.

'Yes... Leicester had a Workers' Education Association, and my written English really came on after a year of studying after work. There was an ulterior motive, of course. There were Poles there, too, and they introduced me to their ex-combatants association. That gave me access to their membership lists, which I searched on the pretext of looking for former comrades. I was able to send back names to Moscow Centre. I felt bad about it, but then I thought about what the Poles had done to my family and thousands of fellow Germans – people who weren't necessarily Nazis, just victims of geography. So I was able to live with it. Having said that, I did think about walking into a police station, or even going to see the Polish government in exile in London. But by then things had gone too far. How would they have treated me, a German and now a traitor to their country?'

'Too risky,' said Gibson. 'They could have been infiltrated by other Soviet agents.'

'As time passed, I began to feel less of an outsider – though I was never made to feel unwelcome. That was also the case with the German PoWs who were working on the local farms. Most of them had been captured in North Africa, and I certainly didn't recognise anyone from Breslau. Ironically I was sometimes "mistaken" for a German, but after a while what anti-German feeling there was faded away. Some of them married English women – I could hardly fault them for doing that – and had decided to stay rather than go back. I know that happened in other parts of the country, too. So it wasn't just the Poles who decided to call this country home. That was one of the things that impressed me about England – most of the people I met were very understanding.

'Liz was devoted to Sophie. She would take her in the pram to go shopping or to Braunstone Park. Our first holiday together as a family was in Nineteen Fifty, when we went on a special excursion to Skegness. That was by train, of course, from the old Belgrave Road station. They were good days... everyone seemed to have a job and there was a strong community spirit. By then I'd become a clerk in the planning department.'

'The classic grey man,' said Gibson.

'Sometimes I'd dream I'd been forgotten about, and that I wouldn't have to lead a double-life anymore... but the Cold War made that impossible. After the Berlin Crisis, the American air forces came back. Then the Korean War started, and by then Russia also had nuclear weapons. Moscow wanted to know what was going on at Cullingthorpe, and other air bases used by American and British bom-bers.' (Thirty years on, he still put the stress on the 'b' in the second syllable.)

'Is that when Todd Casey came into the picture, Dad?'

'Liz talked about him when we were having supper. He'd been back to the chemists a few times by then. She told me how nice he was, how polite he was, and that he seemed a bit homesick. That's when my knife and fork fell on the plate. I told her – shouted at her – to shut up! I couldn't help myself. I was quivering with... what? Guilt? Grief? Fear? A storm was raging inside my head. I'd never raised my voice to her before, so when I said I was going out she just let me go.

'I walked around the park for nearly an hour. By the time she came to find me, I'd made up my mind: I told her... told her everything. When we got back home she poured me a brandy – the only drink we had in the house. She tried to convince me that we could work something out, that if we went to the police, the authorities would take everything into consideration. I always remember what she said to me: "We'll go together... whatever happens I'm not going to leave you.".'

'Then you lost her,' said Gibson.

'Yes... I'd been encoding a message earlier that evening, and expected her to be home by around eight. When she still hadn't arrived half an hour later, I went to find her. Something made me stop near the crossroads. I saw her bike first of all, on the grass verge. The rear wheel was bent horribly out of shape. I shone my torch down into the ditch... and there she was, lying there, staring back at me. I knelt down next to her, took out my handkerchief to clean the mud off her face, then smoothed down her hair. I tried to will her back to life, but it was no use. I closed her eyes...'

Sophie was sat next to her father on the settee. She squeezed his hand and rested her head against his to comfort him.

'I'm sorry to have to ask you this,' said Gibson, clearing his throat, 'but have you been contacted by anyone we should know about – recently, I mean.'

'What else is there to tell? Dad isn't involved in anything now.'

'I haven't been active since her death – that's the truth. There was too much publicity at the time – I was damaged goods. The last message I sent was "Hard Feet" – the code that I'd been compromised. They told me to destroy my set, codebooks, everything.'

'But you didn't,' said Gibson. 'You told us where to find them.'

'And they would have known that long before now... I was offered a new identity, even a passage to Australia. But I wasn't going to change my name again, not for anything. I wanted to stay here... it's what Liz would have wanted. I don't fear a knock on the door anymore, not after all these years. It doesn't matter what happens to me now. I was there for Sophie, that's the main thing.'

'It matters to me, Dad.'

Gibson's pager started beeping.

'Looks like you're wanted,' said Sophie.

He looked at the message, then back at her: 'I won't be long – I just need to make a quick call.'

He found the nearest public phone box.

'Just thought you ought to know,' said Boxted, after picking up on the first ring, 'that a certain Todd Casey is landing at Heathrow tomorrow afternoon. Apparently he's about to turn sixty, the compulsory retirement age for airline pilots.'

'She'll not want to miss him. She might not get another chance.'

'Did her father mention anything of interest to us?'

'He's no longer in the game – I'm certain of that.'

'And what about her? I trust your objectivity is intact?'

'Totally... it will all be in my report.'

Gibson had already convinced himself that Sophie wasn't working for Moscow. But he still had to convince Boxted, and that was going to be more difficult. If Sophie *did* turn out to be an enemy agent, she could be spending the next 20 years in Holloway. It was a prospect he preferred not to think about. Yet if it did happen, he knew in his heart of hearts that he'd be outside the prison gates, waiting for her.

Chapter VI

Segev was sipping chilled orange juice in his hotel room in Madrid. The phone rang. The caller didn't announce himself: 'Don't talk, just listen... meet me across the road at the Museo Sorolla in five minutes. I'll be admiring La Siesta, a fine painting of four young women reposing under a tree. If you don't come my men will arrest you... they are all armed, so I advise you not to try anything.'

Waiting for him was CNI agent Sergio Hernandez. The museum was cool and calm – and public. Much safer than a knock on his hotel door or meeting in the lobby.

Segev carried a Greek passport, but this didn't fool Spain's Centro Nacional de Inteligencia (CNI), who had received word about his departure from Heathrow. They were planning to apprehend a senior member of ETA, and Segev was not welcome. Spain did not recognize the state of Israel, though despite this CNI had received back-channel intelligence relating to links between ETA, the Basque separatist group, and the Palestine Liberation Organisation (PLO).

Hernandez began with a question rather than a greeting: 'What do think of this picture, Señor Segev.'

'My name is –'

'It isn't Peter Karagelis, so don't waste my time by pretending otherwise. We have an ongoing operation against certain individuals, and you're presence here is unhelpful. We don't need your kind of interference.'

The three other CNI agents waiting in the background walked up and stood in a row alongside Hernandez, who then reached inside his jacket pocket: 'A first class ticket to Tel Aviv via Athens. My men will take you to the airport. Have a pleasant flight, Señor.'

Arnold's villa was suitably grand. Positioned at the end of a sweeping drive, it was also well-proportioned, and could have been painted into the landscape. It was sunny and the almond trees were shimmering like burnished silver. The extensive grounds were sprinkled liberally with a variety of other trees, including avocado, fig and lemon. The last mentioned added a hint of citrus to the warm breeze flowing down from the hills.

The CNI had already wired the villa and a surveillance team had quietly taken over one of the few properties that overlooked it. Arnold's guest, Ricardo Ramirez Belasco, was high on the CNI's watch list. He'd been tracked from the arrivals hall at Madrid airport, having flown in from Venezuela on a false Mexican passport under the name of 'Enrique Silva'. He was shopping for weapons, and Arnold was keen to make his first score as a part-time arms dealer. His motivation was purely financial. Not willing to risk rejection by Hollywood, he wanted enough money to green light his own movie. Directing commercials gave him recognition but not fame – and he yearned for both.

His prostitutes came from Los Gatos Rosado in Malaga, a supposedly upmarket establishment run by Lazaro Alvarado, a short, slimy man with permanent stubble and unkempt, tangled hair. Arnold monopolised his two favourites, Lola and Sienna, for days at a time. Alvarado was becoming rich pandering to his client's every demand. Sexual hangups were out – Arnold expected total compliance. Other stipulations included 'No silicone valleys' – and the age limit was strictly 35. Lola was a natural blond – he liked that – and Sienna's hair was long, straight and black – something he also liked.

'Don't wear him out too soon,' said Alvarado, as he drove them up to the villa in his air-conditioned Mercedes.

'He treats us like meat,' said Sienna.

'Worse,' said Lola. 'Even after we fake it he doesn't stop. He's like a beast, like the devil himself.'

As the Mercedes approached the hairpin bend leading up to the villa, they were stopped by troopers of the Guarda Civil. The road was blocked by a line of Land Rover Santanas. He pressed the rocker switch to lower the driver's window: 'Is there a problem?'

'You must stay here, Señor,' announced the nearest trooper.

'But we have important business with Señor Arnold.'

'Not today, Señor.'

'Señor Arnold does not like to be kept waiting.'

'My orders are clear. No one is allowed in or out. No exceptions.'

'Perhaps we could come to some arrangement?' Alvarado reached inside the glove box and pulled out a thick wad of banknotes, which he began to peel off before adding: 'How much do you want?' By this time Capitán Hector Zavala, the local commander, had come over to see what was going on. The troopers stood sharply to attention as Alvarado continued to count off thousands of pesetas...

'Do you think my men can be bought by scum like you?'

Alvarado bundled the money back into the glove box. By now he was sweating profusely. 'I'm sorry if there's been any misunderstanding, Capitán...'

'The only reason I'm not turning you over to the local police is because I have more pressing matters to attend to.'

'Please forgive me, Capitán... we'll be on our way.'

'You're not going anywhere until I say so – I don't want you calling the house. Better for you, better for the two charming señoritas.' They smiled as he touched the brim of his cap, then wiggled their fingers at him before he turned away.

'The Capitán is very handsome,' said Sienna.

'We still have other customers,' snapped Alvarado. 'I had to put off the skipper from that Russian cargo ship this morning. He won't pay as much as Señor Arnold, but business is business.'

'Both of us?' asked Lola.

'One of his officers wants some action, too.'

'Let's hope the air-conditioning works,' continued Lola, 'or we'll fry in that big steel oven.'

'Would you prefer going back to screwing in alleyways? And what about your nice, rent-free apartment? Who else is going to look after you, eh?'

'We might get lucky one day,' said Sienna, wistfully.

As she spoke, Zavala returned to his vehicle to take an urgent radio message: 'Capitán, we have a target on the move.'

The surveillance team had heard Belasco agree a price for the first consignment. He and Arnold were now under the portico of the villa, their handshakes and backslapping captured by cameras buzzing on motor drive.

Belasco set off down the winding drive in his hired SEAT 128. Arnold gave him a final wave as the car descended out of view. *The girls should be here by now*, he thought. *What's keeping them?* A group of rufous bush robins were busily hopping around in the scrub that surrounded the gardens. Their mournful song was interrupted not by the sound of Alvarado's Mercedes, but by the unmistakable chatter of machine guns in fully automatic mode.

The shots echoed sharply around the valley. Belasco had declined to stop at the roadblock, and had somehow managed to survive the bullets aimed at both him and his vehicle. Back he came up the hill, weaving crazily in a cloud of dust. Three Land Rovers, headlights on full beam, blue lights flashing, were following. Arnold could only watch dumbfounded as Belasco tumbled out of the bullet-riddled SEAT. He'd been hit more than once, and the slug lodged in his right forearm forced him to hold his Beretta 9mm automatic left-handed.

'You set me up, didn't you?'

'No! Never! Please – don't shoot!'

The first bullet took Arnold just below the left shoulder. Four more followed, ripping into his heart and lungs. He collapsed, coughing up blood. The transmission whine of the leading Land Rover ended abruptly as Zavala jumped out, his Star Z-70b submachine gun at the ready. He did not feel the need to offer Belasco the option of surrendering. Instead he cocked his weapon with a slick double-click – it was almost the last sound that Belasco, half-dead, half-blinded by the unyielding glare of the sun, would hear. A short burst nailed him to the ground.

Zavala said two words over him: 'Adios, bastardo...' And then the rufous bush robins resumed their mournful song.

Chapter VII

Gibson and Sophie were now back on the M1, southbound. 'You've gone quiet again,' she said. 'Is anything wrong?'

'No... just thinking about tomorrow.'

'It must be important...'

'Well, for one thing, Todd Casey will be coming through Arrivals at Heathrow…'

'Really? Can I see him?'

'That's the plan... though it might be better if I speak to him first. We don't know how he's going to react...'

'Yes… he may not want to talk to me.'

'We'll find out soon enough.'

'Isn't this all a bit extracurricular?'

'It's no bother, believe me. You know, I wouldn't mind talking to your dad again sometime. What he had to say was fascinating. That's the sort of history you rarely find in books.'

'I'm glad you were there. He really enjoyed meeting you, too – and that's more than can be said for most of the men I've brought home. You haven't said much about your family…'

'It might send you to sleep.'

'It can't be *that* boring.'

'Well, both my parents had good jobs before they decided to retire. Dad was in a maritime insurance syndicate at Lloyd's, just like his father before him. Mum worked as an occupational therapist. We lived in Bromley in a modern detached house with a double garage – I suppose you could say we were comfortably off. I was born two years after my sister, Sue.'

'Do you see much of them?'

'Not really. Sue moved to Melbourne before I joined the Marines. She started off as a nurse at one of the big London Teaching Hospitals – Guy's, I think – and I remember her coming home with a stack of forms and brochures from Australia House. Mum cried her eyes out when she told her she was emigrating. I was glad to see the back of her, to be honest. She tried to boss me around too much, so I kicked back. Mum always took her side, and Dad always backed her up. I didn't become a loner, exactly, but I often went straight to my room after supper. When I got my Sturmey Archer three-speed bike I would be off on that until it was nearly dark.'

'Didn't they take any interest in you at all?'

'Mum and I became closer when she realised that Sue wasn't coming back. But Dad was always something of a cold fish. All that seemed to matter to him was money. He worked damned hard, I'll give him that. Now he lives on the golf course.'

'What did he do in the war?'

'Touchy subject. When I joined the CCF at school, he decided to take me down to Lloyd's in the school holidays. I saw him writing the insurance for a cargo ship, and he gave me the "one day, all this will be yours" speech. I just wasn't interested. On the way home, I told him I wasn't cut out for it – or words to that effect. He wasn't exactly pleased. He was even less pleased when I said I wanted to join the army. I remember the stony silence. Eventually he said: "Make sure you train for a trade, there'll be nothing for you on the outside if you go into the infantry". He'd been a quartermaster in the RASC – what the Americans call "in the rear with the beer". He must have thought that wasn't impressive enough.

'Your dad knew all about the importance of logistics, of course. If you haven't got enough food, ammo, fuel and all the other things in the right place, at the right time, you're going to lose. I didn't think any less of Dad for his service – he did a vital job. I just wish he'd been a bit more encouraging, that's all.'

Gibson waited a minute or two before he spoke again. 'Can I see you – when this is all over, I mean.'

'You're asking me out?'

'We could have a few drinks –'

'Oh yes? And then what?'

'Nothing – if that's what you want. Or you can come sailing with me sometime. You can always dive over the side if I start to bore the hell out of you. Judging by all your cups and medals, you'd probably get back to shore before I did.'

'There's a good chance I'll stay on board – unless we hit a rock or something.'

'It isn't a yacht, just a sailboat, a Shark 24, over at Hayling Island. She's laid up at the moment, but all she really needs is a new spinnaker and a good clean up.'

'I think you should know any cleaning I do begins and ends in my own flat.'

'Don't get me wrong – I wouldn't expect you to help. I'll make sure she's shipshape and Bristol fashion.'

'This is your private passion, I take it?'

'I took it up again after going through a bad patch. I learned the ropes in Corsica after a group of us got chatting to an instructor in one of the bars in Ajaccio. I started in a dinghy, then graduated to a thirty-six footer. We'd charter one and sail round until it was time to find a beach and go for a beer. The seafood was incredibly good – we'd feast on seabream, red mullet, or – best of all – John Dory, usually just cooked in foil with a dash of good olive oil.'

'Fish and chips must seem a bit tame after that.'

'Not with a bottle of chardonnay, nicely chilled, of course.'

'I'll have to try that sometime. Would you ever go back?'

'Permanently, you mean?'

'No, just for a holiday – it sounds idyllic.'

'I hate to change the subject, but I think we're being followed.'

'Are you sure.'

'Two chaps in a black Capri, about three cars back.'

'How long has it been there?'

'About ten minutes or so. We'll pull in at the next services. Let's see if they follow.'

Gibson was now fully alert. They pulled into Northampton services and found a space about ten yards from a row of telephone boxes. Gibson reversed-parked his Carlton. The Capri parked up two rows behind them.

'Perhaps there's someone else on my case, Gary?'

'You could be right...'

'What are you going to do?'

'I'm going to call Boxted. In case anything happens, I want you to drive round to the petrol station and call the police.' As he unfastened his seat belt, she held him back for a moment: 'Be careful.'

She looked at the Capri. The men were now outside. Suits. Sunglasses. Trouble. They were walking like they were made of steel, as if nothing could touch them. One was about 25, medium build, and clean cut. The other was much older – 40-plus, thick set and with the face of a boxer who had had one fight too many. When Gibson stepped into the phone box, the older man headed straight towards him. As he did so his right hand reached inside his jacket. The next thing Sophie saw was the glint of a chrome-plated Colt .45 automatic.

As he closed to point blank range, she sounded the horn – one long, continuous note of urgency. Gibson turned round. In the split-second before the gunman fired, he booted open the door. The bullet hit the frame, sending a shower of glass across the pavement – and at the gunman, who instinctively tried to protect himself. That gave Gibson the chance to make a grab for the gun. But his opponent was strong and tough. As they struggled, Gibson was taking some vicious punches to the head and body.

The second man then started to run towards them. Sophie put the Carlton into first gear and mashed the accelerator to the floor. As he turned towards her, the front bumper took him off his feet. He went across the bonnet, up and over the windscreen, then slid across the roof and back down to the ground. It was a knockout blow. His left shin bone was projecting through the skin at a grotesque angle – a severe and shocking injury. But it was the snub-nosed Smith & Wesson .38 that had spilled from his right hand that caught her attention. She dashed over to retrieve it

Gibson's assailant was still trying to throw him off and finish the job. Sophie advanced, holding the revolver in a two-handed, combat grip. She could feel her heart pounding with every single step. Gibson was weakening. After taking another punch in the stomach, he spun away. Three shots came in quick succession. They were from Sophie, and her shooting was deadly accurate. As the gunman dropped to his knees, he somehow managed to fire again. Fortunately the bullet ricocheted harmlessly into the front grille of a parked BMW. Gibson, somewhat unsteady on his feet, went over to him and tried to feel for a pulse that wasn't there. As Sophie came up to him, Gibson was taking off his jacket to cover the man's face.

'He would've killed you... I had no choice,' she said.

'All the same I think you'd better give me that.' She handed over the gun, butt first, safety on. Seconds later a Rover 3.5 V8 from the traffic division of Northamptonshire Police pulled up alongside, headlights and blue lights flashing.

Gibson showed the sergeant his Home Office warrant card: 'She's with me. You'll need to contact Special Branch.'

The sergeant nodded. 'We're not used to this sort of thing.'

'We thought it was just a car backfiring at first,' added the second traffic officer.

'He's had it,' said Gibson, looking towards the deceased.

'The other one's still with us,' said Sophie. 'I'll need a first aid kit, some blankets and some kind of splint for his leg.'

The sergeant was more interested in the gun Gibson was holding. 'Shall I take that off your hands, sir?'

'It's on safe, but still loaded. There's another one – an automatic – next to the body.'

The sergeant put his pen through the trigger guard and placed the gun inside an evidence bag. 'We'll leave the other one where it is for the time being,' said the sergeant. 'All we can do now is try and secure the scene as best we can until the CID boys arrive.'

Both officers then began to clear away the bystanders in the immediate vicinity. 'If anyone saw anything,' said the sergeant, 'please wait in the cafeteria. We'll need statements from you before you leave. The rest of you can go about your business.'

'Are you in charge here?'

The sergeant looked up. He was being addressed by a middle-aged man in a pinstriped suit, the smartness of which was rather undermined by an exaggerated comb-over that kept lifting in the breeze at irregular intervals. 'My BMW's been damaged.'

'Did you see what happened, sir?'

'No. I did not. I'm a chartered accountant, and I happen to have an urgent appointment with the Lord Lieutenant of the county. I only stopped to answer a call of nature.'

'This is now a crime scene. Your car will have to be taken away for examination.'

'But what about my appointment?'

'You'll just have to make alternative arrangements.'

'Can't you take me there? I'll have you know that the Lord Lieutenant is a close personal friend of the Chief Constable.'

'We're not a taxi service, though I'm sure a local firm will be able to oblige. Now, if you don't mind, I've got more important things to attend to.'

'Don't think you've heard the last of this.' There was an audible huff. 'Not by a long chalk.' He then turned on his heels and went to retrieve a portfolio briefcase from the BMW.

Meanwhile, Sophie was treating the surviving gunman – he was in a bad way. After handing her the first aid kit from the Rover, the other traffic officer began folding up some stiff cardboard for the splint.

'You seem to know what you're doing,' he said.

'He really needs a doctor... we'll just have to do the best we can for him.'

The man's breathing was very laboured, and he was going into shock. She managed to stop the bleeding by applying bandages, and wasted no time in covering up the exposed bone with a sterile dressing. Then the ambulance arrived, together with another three police cars. The ambulance men took over, and she went back to Gibson – with the first aid kit.

'What happens now?' she asked, busily cleaning up a nasty cut above his right eye.

He grimaced: 'I'd better make that phone call.'

Boxted could hardly believe his ears. Security Service officers aren't supposed to be shot at in broad daylight. For the second time in a week he was on the phone to a high court judge and a chief constable, explaining why their identities had to be kept out of the public domain. The legal advice was clear: Sophie had acted in self-defence and with 'reasonable force'. The second gunman had died in the ambulance on the way to hospital – an autopsy would reveal the exact cause of death. The only possible charge against Sophie would be that of manslaughter, though Boxted was assured that the Director of Public Prosecutions (DPP), would probably regard a trial as 'not in the public interest'. In the meantime, she was released pending further enquiries. Both of them would have to appear at the inquest in due course, albeit behind a screen.

As they were driven back to London by Special Branch, Gibson had plenty of time to process what had happened and come to a few conclusions. He reckoned the attempted hit was a rush job. The trigger men were too sloppy, too eager. A chrome-plated .45? Not the sort of thing a professional would carry – including anyone from an IRA active service unit. No: they must have come from gangland, acting as proxies with the promise of a big pay day. Whoever hired them wasn't too fussy. That wouldn't have mattered had he been travelling alone. He knew he would now be lying on a slab had Sophie not acted immediately. Her coolness under the most intense pressure imaginable had been extraordinary. Boxted had already told him she was a winner with a pistol – but shooting to kill is not the same as putting holes in a paper target.

Sir Stephen had not gone home until Scotland Yard had confirmed the identity of the gunmen, namely Barry 'Bud' Flanagan (42) and Derek Reece (33). As Gibson had surmised, they were career criminals, East End enforcers with records longer than Waterloo Bridge – but few convictions. The Capri carried false plates and had been reported stolen from Brent Cross shopping centre the week before. Ballistic reports on the guns they carried would soon reveal if the bullets matched those recovered from the bodies of several possible victims.

As to the source, Sir Stephen had his suspicions, which is why he had spoken to 'C', his opposite number at SIS, who had to be called out of a meeting at Chequers. 'C' assured him that 'everything possible' would be done to assist in the search for answers. He was, however, busy briefing the PM on the implications of a major arms sale to one of the Gulf states, and would be staying for dinner. Reluctant to discuss the matter further until he had returned to London, he accepted Sir Stephen's invitation to a working lunch the following day.

After dropping Sophie off in Bermondsey, it was 7.00pm by the time Gibson arrived at Gower Street. 'Are you sure you're alright?' asked Boxted.

'Just about... I wouldn't be here at all if it hadn't been for –'

'I realise that. Sir Stephen wanted me to pass on his deep concern. He was barely able to contain his anger.'

'I wasn't exactly thrilled about it myself.'

'At least you're still alive. That's more than can be said for Tony Arnold. I believe you've met?'

'I thought he was supposed to be in Spain?'

'SIS passed on a flash from our embassy in Madrid. This afternoon he was shot dead by one Ricardo Ramirez Belasco, a senior commander of ETA. Belasco was about to be arrested, and it looks like he thought Arnold – rightly or wrongly – had fingered him. At the moment that's merely conjecture – the Guarda Civil didn't take him alive.'

'Was anyone running Arnold?'

'I doubt it was SIS – they tipped off the CNI. Arnold was too much of a loose cannon for my taste. Others may not have been so picky. You know, you really ought to rest up for a few days…'

'I don't want Sophie to miss the chance of meeting Todd Casey.'

'Somehow I knew you were going to say that.'

Chapter VIII

At 7.00am, Sophie listened to a speculative report on the incident on Radio 4. At her local newsagents, the headlines in the red tops were predictably colourful. The splash 'ANNIE' GETS HER GUN – TWO DEAD IN M1 SHOOTOUT was typical. It featured an artist's impression of her firing at the first gunman that could have come straight from the pages of a Marvel comic book. Her name – and Gibson's – were conspicuously absent. Their identities were 'unknown' but a 'reliable Scotland Yard source' had suggested they could have been 'police officers working undercover'.

The 'reliable Scotland Yard source' had been primed by Boxted. He had also anticipated the connection a certain DI Copeland and his crew would make when they saw the story. And he also had to be sure Drusilla Williams would keep any similar thoughts to herself. He saw a way of dealing with the situation in one fell swoop.

As soon as Copeland rolled into work – somewhat the worse for wear after too many doubles in the Horse & Jockey – the duty sergeant beckoned him over. 'Urgent message from Special Branch. You're to call this number right away.'

'Not again, for pity's sake. It's too early in the morning.'

'It's nearly ten o'clock, sir.'

'I make it nearer eight-thirty… my watch must have stopped.'

He half-stumbled into his office and dialled. WPC Keeley had seen it all before. She was soon making him a coffee, strong and black with three sugars. The head of Special Branch, no less, was on the other end of the line. He had been briefed by Boxted, and what he had to say made Copeland sober up – though Keeley's coffee certainly helped. Chief Superintendent David Matthews had already been put in the picture, he was told. The rest was up to him: 'Just leave it to me, sir.'

He rallied his troops – namely MacDonald, Stevenson and Keeley – and, after bolting his beverage, took them out into the car park. He came straight to the point: 'If a certain name happens to get out, all the shit in creation will be heading in our direction. I don't know about you, but I'm damned if I'm going to lose my pension over this.'

'We've all seen the papers,' said Stevenson.

'The word is they were working undercover,' added MacDonald. 'Do you reckon that's true, guv?'

'There's stuff going on here that we'll never get to know about. All that matters now is that we keep a lid on this – starting with that cabbie at the airport. Find him, play up the undercover angle, thank him for his cooperation. Don't say anything you don't have to. If that doesn't work, just say I'll be paying him a personal visit, after hours. The last thing we need is some scumbag reporter calling at Williams' place. I'm going over to see her with young Keeley here. You can drop us off first and then pick us up when you've finished with whatshisname.'

It wasn't long before he was rapping the knocker at 27 Olympic Avenue. The door opened slightly. 'Not today, thank you,' said Mrs Williams. His size 10 was already in the door. 'Police,' he said, 'Detective Inspector Copeland.'

She led them into the living room, and he adopted his usual direct approach: 'Seen this?'

He handed her one of the morning editions. She took in the headline – GUN GIRL KILLS TWO – then looked back at him. 'Are you saying – ?'

'I'm not saying anything, love. And neither are you.'

He parked himself on the settee, uninvited.

'She was here a few days ago, sat where you are now, my niece, my own kith and kin. I wouldn't do anything to harm her.'

'I'd sit down too if I were you, love.' She took one of the armchairs, while Keeley sat next to him. 'Good at keeping secrets are you, Mrs Williams?' His tone was matter-of-fact, but with a distinct edge to it.

She paused before answering. It was a nervous pause: 'How much do you know?'

'Let's start with the gun.'

'Oh no…'

He heaved himself up to give her a cigarette. Their eyes met as he lit it. The hunter and the hunted. She went over to open one of the bay windows. 'I don't normally smoke in the house, you know.'

'We've checked your hubbies service record. He was posted to Korea... and he came back with a little souvenir, didn't he?'

'He thought he was so clever, hiding it in some aircraft spares.'

'Why didn't you hand it in when you had the chance?'

'Gordon said he was going to, then changed his mind. I could hardly make him, could I? In the end he just decided to hide it. When that fella came round with Sophie, I was able to get shut of it once and for all.'

'Well, that's one less thing to worry about.'

'There's something else... something I'm not very proud of.'

'Come on then, love – get it off your chest. This is just between the three of us, I promise you that.'

'All I wanted was a baby, a kid of my own to care for.'

Normally any attempt to elicit sympathy from Copeland would be like trying to melt an iceberg with a sunlamp. Keeley hardly needed her female intuition to know that his interest in Mrs Williams seemed to be progressing beyond the needs of normal police work.

'There was nothing wrong with me... not until my first bit of fun with a fella. He kept buying me drinks, and, well... he took advantage, didn't he? I was only seventeen – trying to grow up too fast. I was just starting to show when I went to this backstreet abortionist. Butcher, more like. I went to a gynaecologist after I married... we were trying for a baby. That's when I found out I was barren. Then Liz came to see me with Sophie...

'We met in the station buffet at Lime Street. Mum and Dad just didn't want to know – they'd never forgiven her for eloping – but I'd always admired her for it.

'Her baby was so beautiful, so perfect. But I could see Liz was troubled. At first I thought she just had the blues. Then she told me about Dominik flying off the handle, that he was some kind of spy. So when she died I put two and two together. I worked myself up into a right old state, convinced myself that he'd killed her – that's why I blanked him at the funeral. I thought he'd go down, that I'd get custody...'

'You've had to live with this for far too long,' said Keeley.

'It's too late for tears, pet. At least Gordon and me had some good years together. We were fine until he took that job in Korea. He'd never expected to go back there, but they needed a manager for one of their new car plants. He jumped at it – I guess the blood wasn't quite so warm by then. He used to fly home every six weeks, said the job would only last a year, if that. It paid off the mortgage, so after that I didn't have to work full-time. I went temping with an agency, for the social side as much as anything. Then he sent me a letter, said he'd met someone else. I gave him his divorce. He gave me the house and some cash in the bank. So here I am, the wrong side of fifty and on the shelf.'

'I'd count your blessings if I were you, love. I'm divorced too, and my daughter's shacked up with some long-haired Trot who likes to give coppers the Nazi salute. She hasn't spoken to me for years. He's poisoned her mind.'

'Well, I suppose we all have our troubles, don't we?' said Mrs Williams, tapping the ash from her cigarette out the window.

'Didn't you want to go back to your maiden name?' asked Keeley.

'Not really, pet. I decided to stick with Williams because my maiden name is Hagg. And I don't want to end up being an old Hagg, do I?'

'There's not much chance of that happening,' said Copeland, chuckling. Keeley couldn't help but laugh herself. 'I'd say you're still in your prime,' he continued. 'Any man would be proud to have you on his arm, me included.'

'I believe you, thousands wouldn't. The bloke who came with Sophie said the same, more or less.'

'I've met him – too clever by half if you ask me. I put him back in his box alright, I can tell you. Then I made sure she was okay. I sorted everything out for her, you know.'

'That was good of you. I don't suppose you've got time for some tea and biscuits?' She had finished her cigarette, and smoothed her hands down her waist like a contestant in a beauty pageant.

'I thought you'd never ask,' he said, his mouth a little on the dry side. Without taking his eyes off her, he sat back with his hands behind his head and crossed his feet as she made her way to the kitchen. Keeley grinned, shaking her head slowly.

Heathrow Airport, 2.02pm

Gibson was in Arrivals in Terminal 3 when he spotted the man he'd been waiting for. 'Captain Casey? I'm with the Home Office.' He flashed his ID. 'Could I have a word with you... in private?'

'We'll just go on ahead to the hotel,' said his first officer.

'Is this going to take long? We're having a little celebration tonight. Tomorrow will be my last flight as captain.'

'I won't keep you a second longer than I really need to. Did you have a good trip?'

'We had a one hundred and fifty knot tailwind most of the way, so we came in way ahead of schedule.'

Casey was ushered towards an anonymous looking door near passport control. 'Has something happened back home,' he asked, 'to my wife?'

'No... it's something else.'

'Did my crew put you up to this? Is this a gag?'

'It's about Elizabeth Zoborski.'

There was a long pause before Casey replied. 'I don't have to say anything to anyone. I'm a US citizen.'

Hearing her name again had clearly unsettled him.

Gibson pressed on: 'I'm here on behalf of her only child, Sophie. All she wants to do is talk to you.'

Casey took off his cap, then brought out a handkerchief to mop his brow. 'Jesus H Christ...'

'Can I get you a glass of water?'

'I'm gonna need something stronger than that... I guess I've had this thing hanging over me long enough. Let's go.'

Gibson led him into a private room with two armchairs and a couple of matching dark brown leather settees either side of a glass coffee table. Sophie was standing at the single window, double-glazed to dull the jet noise.

'Are you really Sophie?' asked Casey, nervously.

'Thank you for agreeing to meet me.'

Casey's handshake was decidedly limp. He was transfixed. It was as though he'd seen her before, which, in a way, he had.

'Won't you sit down?' said Sophie.

'What would you like to drink?' asked Gibson.

'Bourbon, if you've got any.'

'What about a single malt?'

'Sure. Why not?'

'Any ice... or water?'

'Just water... but don't drown it.'

'Sophie?'

'I'll keep you company. Just ice with mine, please.'

'I think I'll follow suit.' Gibson made a call from the wall-mounted phone and within a few minutes there was a knock at the door. Everything he'd ordered was on a tray, which he placed on the table.

When Casey tried to pick up his glass, he nearly dropped it. 'Kinda heavy, aren't they?'

Gibson smiled: 'Lead crystal.'

'Did you ever go drinking with Elizabeth?' asked Sophie.

'We certainly never went to any bars, if that's what you mean. I'd say she was practically teetotal.'

'How did you meet?'

'She worked in the local drug store...'

'You mean the chemists?'

'Sometimes I forget we're two nations divided by a common language. I went in there one day for some aspirin. I didn't want to go to the pharmacy on base because if the doc got to hear of it... well, he could've grounded me.'

'And you kept on seeing her?'

'The headaches passed – just a little eye strain, I guess – but I kept buying aspirin. I soon had enough for the whole outfit.'

'But you knew she was married?'

'Liz was a sweet girl – though she was nobody's fool. I guess I fell for her, but she wasn't going to be unfaithful – no way. If I wasn't rostered for a mission, I'd try to drive over and meet her for lunch. She liked to eat her sandwiches on a little bridge over the river. We enjoyed each other's company. The time passed very quickly...'

Sophie smiled. 'Did you ever see me?'

105

'This is definitely the first time... though Liz did talk about you.'

'Can you remember the last time you saw her?'

'You'll need to fix me another drink.' Gibson obliged. 'We used to drink this stuff after every mission. It wasn't as good as this, though. This is real smooth.'

'So you were over here in the war?'

'Over here is right, buddy. Twenty-three missions in B-17s. Never got a scratch. We were luckier than the guys who came over when the Eighth Air Force was building up. There were no Schweinfurts for us. We came over in the fall of Nineteen Forty-Four, and I flew my last combat mission in April Forty-Five. No fighters, just light flak, mostly. We plastered a crossroads in some godforsaken town I'd never heard of. A walk in the park.'

'They can't all have been as easy as that,' said Gibson.

'Pretty much – though one of the squadrons in our group got wiped out – I mean, nobody came back. And we're talking February Forty-Five here, when the Luftwaffe was supposed to be finished. The dope was they'd run into some of the new jet jobs – Me 262s – and they wouldn't have stood a chance.'

'Did you bring back any souvenirs?'

'Not that I recall. Some of the guys came back with all sorts of stuff. Lugers were highly prized. I had a service-issue Browning automatic that I never even bothered to clean, let alone shoot. I think it only came out of the holster twice, and the second time was when the sergeant checked the serial number when I handed it back in.'

'I was asking you about the last time you saw my Mum?'

'Sorry, Sophie,' said Gibson. 'My fault.'

'That's okay – it's all very interesting.'

Casey continued: 'There's something I oughta mention first. Apparently our meetings hadn't gone unnoticed. One day my CO called me into his office, and what he had to say made my head spin. He said Liz's husband had come to the attention of our MPs. He'd become a regular at the perimeter fence, and something about him must have aroused suspicion. At that time our B-36s were making regular deployments from the States.'

'He was a Soviet agent before he came over to us after his wife's death,' said Gibson.

106

'That figures. I was flying KB-29s at that time, the ships we used for air-refuelling – that was no big secret. We usually waved at the plane spotters as we taxied past... most of them were schoolboys. I guess it was good for community relations.'

'He would have noted the aircraft type, number of sorties flown, duration, et cetera,' said Gibson. 'Useful information for Soviet intelligence.'

'You sure didn't need to hide in the woods with a pair of binoculars. Our B-36s were huge – just about the biggest airplane in the world at that time.'

'They must have been an impressive sight.'

'They sure were – especially on take-off. The B-36 was real heavy, and we had to extend the main runway before we were declared combat ready.'

'Did your CO mention anything else?' asked Sophie.

'He wanted to know if I'd ever talked to Liz about what we were doing over here. "Did I realise they could be working as a team?" I straightened him out on that point, right there. I do recall throwing in a few profanities along the way... which didn't go down too well. He chewed me out, said I was way out of line, that he couldn't take any chances. He was going to do me a favour by re-assigning me to a training wing in Florida, my home state, for conversion to the B-47 – our latest jet bomber. I was dumb enough to think I could have it all – Liz, a big house, promotion, everything. I had to speak to her, so as soon as I could, I took a jeep and drove into the village. I didn't know she was working late that evening, and it was a quarter after seven by the time she came out.'

His mind flashed back to April 1953...

'What are you doing here?'

It was Elizabeth.

'It's starting to rain. Let me put your bike in the jeep.'

There was hardly any traffic on the roads. Soon they were quite alone, driving along the B road that led to the small Norman church at Leckenby. 'I guess this is as good a place as any.' Casey pulled over. The church stood guard in the strong moonlight. The branches of nearby trees swayed and creaked as the wind and rain continued to sweep over them.

'This is a bit creepy, Todd, don't you think?'

'You have to listen to me, Liz. I know that you're married to a commie spy – do you have any idea what that means?'

'That's not fair. It wasn't his fault.'

'How can you live under the same roof – with a kid?'

'Dom has told me everything, how he was forced into it. We're going to go to the authorities... we're going to try and make a clean breast of it.'

'He's bound to be put on trial – for treason. Any attorney worth his salt will tear him apart. He could hang for what he's done. And you'd be an accessory after the fact. You could spend your best years in prison.'

'When Dom and I got married –'

'Don't tell me – for better, for worse, for richer, for poorer...'

'I have to stand by him.'

'Who do you think you are for Christ's sake? Joan of Arc? You're throwing your life away...'

'You don't know that...'

'Hear me out, Liz. There is an alternative – come with me to the States. Just think of the quality of life over there. Think of the kid...'

'I am thinking of Sophie... and Dom is a good man, a kind man. We're going to see this through, even if it means going to the highest court in the land. After this is over he can go to night school and get more qualifications. Sophie will start going to school soon, and I'll be able to work in the chemists more or less full-time. I've been watching the pharmacist, and I know I can do his job. I just need to study and pass the exams.'

'You're a bright girl. So why can't you see what I'm laying out for you here? I'm up for promotion, and that comes with generous pay and allowances. We can live comfortably – no more rationing, no more of this make-do-and-mend stuff. You won't need a bicycle over there – we'll have a sedan or a station wagon. The kid will go to a good school and you'll never have to worry about food, clothing or healthcare – the Air Force looks after its own.'

'I like you, Todd, but that's as far as it goes. I'm sorry – I know you're only trying to help...'

'America is the future, Liz. This place is no better than it was during the war…'

'But this is our home. And things *are* getting better. A bit too slowly for you it seems, but getting better all the same. We get all the care we need from the Health Service, and we don't have to worry about the cost. If things work out we'll soon have a new council house…'

'I didn't mean to be disrespectful. I like England, too. Sure I do.'

'Then why can't you understand?'

'Because I'm crazy about you.'

'Look, Todd. You're bound to meet someone else. They'll be lots of nice girls over there...'

'Not like you.'

'My life is with Dom, and, try as you might, you can never be a part of it. I'm sorry – nothing is going to change that.'

'Well, I guess I've given it my best shot… can I write you?'

'Of course you can. Look, I really must be getting home now.'

'…Captain Casey… Captain Casey... are you okay?' It was Gibson bringing him back to the here and now.

'Sorry... I was thinking about –'

'The last time you saw my Mum.'

'You know, even after all this time I can still see her tying up her headscarf and giving me that cute little smile of hers. She gave me a final wave and then stepped on the pedals. I watched her rear light until it became a tiny speck in the distance. I was just about to start the jeep when an old army truck pulled up and the driver got out to ask for directions. He wasn't exactly loaded, but I could tell he'd had a few drinks. I knew Liz would be turning left at the end of the road, and I figured she'd be too far ahead to be in any danger. That's what I told the police. I wish I'd noticed the number of the truck. I wish I'd never gone to meet her... When I saw the story in the paper my guts turned inside out. It was the worst day of my life.'

'The driver of the truck never came forward,' said Gibson, 'so we'll probably never know what happened in those final moments.'

'What happened, happened,' said Sophie. I wouldn't hold yourself responsible in any way.'

A thought beyond time, driven by compassion, made her embrace him. Then she kissed him on the cheek.

'You're good people. Sorry, I'm kinda choked up.'

She handed him her handkerchief, and he dabbed his eyes with it. 'I guess I really loved her – just don't mention it to my wife. Confession may be good for the soul, but I'm not convinced it's good for a happy marriage.'

'Your secret is safe with me,' she said.

'Say, are you two –?'

'We just work together,' said Gibson, determined to get in first.

Sophie smiled: 'I think we've kept you for long enough.'

'It's been no trouble, believe me. I feel as though I've finally put things straight. If you're ever in Miami, be sure to look me up. Here's my card, Sophie – you can call me anytime.'

'Thank you – I'll certainly take you up on that when I get the chance.'

'That goes for you too, buddy.'

He handed over another card to Gibson. 'You know, something's been bothering me about you. What happened to your face?'

'Ah yes – it was a glass door.'

'You walked into it?'

'Something like that…'

They poured him into a taxi at Arrivals, then waved goodbye.

'Strange to think you could have been his stepdaughter.'

'Maybe I am – in another life. Better than being brought up by Drusilla Williams, anyway.'

'I think you ought to know that Tony Arnold's now in the next world, wherever that is.'

'What happened? Did he –'

'Someone shot him dead at his villa.'

'Normally I wouldn't wish that on anybody, but in his case…'

'I didn't think you'd be too broken up about it.'

'Just as a matter of interest, do we know who did it?'

'The details are still sketchy. Sorry, but I need to go now. I have a little job to do at West Midlands Airport.'

'Official business?'

'There's another Russian cargo flight coming in tomorrow – nothing to get excited about. The crew usually head straight for the duty free shop. That's about all there is to it.'

'I think I'll call the office. Sandy might need some moral support. Thanks again for everything.'

'I'll pass that on to Boxted. He did all the leg work.'

'Please do... and take care of yourself.'

After giving him a parting peck on the cheek, she went back into the terminal to use a payphone.

Like Sophie, Georgie was far from upset about Arnold's death. 'It's Sandy I feel sorry for.'

'Is he there?' asked Sophie.

'No – he flew out this morning to identify the body.'

Malaga, 3.30pm

First stop for Johnson was the Garda Civil. He was met by Capitán Zavala. 'Please accept my condolences, Señor. I take it he was a good friend of yours?'

'Thank you. Yes, he was. I still can't believe he's dead. What on earth happened?'

'It is a complicated affair – the investigation will take many months to complete. What we know for certain is that he was shot by a terrorist –'

'A *terrorist?*'

'Yes, Señor.'

'What was it... a case of mistaken identity?'

'Regrettably, I have to say that Señor Arnold was dealing with some very dangerous people.'

'I just don't understand it... he'd only just moved out here... he had everything to live for...'

'This must be difficult for you, but we need to make the identification as soon as possible. The mortuary is not far from here. Come, I will escort you.'

After a brief word with the attendant, Zavala beckoned Johnson into an air-conditioned room. The white tiles on the walls gleamed under the glow of fluorescent tubes, one of which was flickering intermittently.

The body was on a trolley, covered with a plain white sheet. The attendant drew back it back to reveal the face. At first Johnson thought it must be someone else. Arnold appeared to have aged at least twenty years. It was as though the life had been sucked out of him. And his contorted features revealed all too clearly the pain he had suffered in his death throes.

'So is it Arnold?' asked Zavala.

'Yes... I'm afraid it is. What were you thinking of, Tony? You stupid, bloody fool...'

'Señor Johnson, please.'

'I'm sorry... it's just such a bloody waste.'

'There are just a few formalities, then you can go.'

When Johnson stepped outside, the heat of the street enveloped him like a woollen blanket. He could hear Spanish guitar music filtering down from an upstairs window. Zavala was listening, too. 'Rodrigo, Señor. It's called Tiento Antiguo. A difficult piece to master... it needs to be played from the heart.'

'It's beautiful, isn't it? If you don't mind, I think I'll just stay here for a while...'

Chapter IX

East Berlin, Friday, 24th June, 9.30am

It was time to begin the final briefing for Operation VIKTOR. 'Let's close the curtains and have some lights,' said Koslov. A guard had been posted at the door. The atmosphere was heavy with anticipation. He picked up a pointer and slid back a large screen. Behind it was a series of overlapping photographs taken from the glazed nose section of Major Ostapenko's An-12 on its first visit to West Midlands Airport. 'England... East Anglia. We'll be picking up the special package from here, Cullingthorpe, a disused bomber airfield that's almost on a direct track from the airport. Some old farm equipment has been dumped on the western end of the runway, but that still leaves us with just under two thousand metres to play with. The package only weighs four hundred kilograms, so even with full fuel we'll be comparatively light. I think you'll all agree that's much better than coaxing a fully-laden aircraft out of a hot-and-high dirt strip in Afghanistan.' His wry smile lightened the mood among his crew – but it had no effect on Belyakov or Malenkovich. They were not part of the brotherhood.

'Although marked as disused, it's still visited occasionally by their air force and special forces. Now you might think that would be a good reason for avoiding it, but our information is that it's rarely used, and then almost always at night. Another thing in its favour is that it's relatively remote – the nearest town is nearly four kilometres away. We also have special forces, and we need to think as they do – audaciously. Two comrades – another from the spetsnaz and a torpedo specialist from the Northern Fleet – will be waiting for us.

We'll be using the same An-12 as before. Same callsign, same route, same everything – that is until we land at Cullingthorpe. As part of the plan to disguise our intentions, we'll pretend to have a radio failure. So we'll fly a left-hand orbit before dropping down below their radar cover. Time is our biggest enemy, especially when we're on the ground. We must be up and away before their air force can react. Even if they do, we'll soon be in international airspace –

and untouchable. After that it should simply be a case of cruising up the North Sea and around the North Cape. Our mission ends when the package is unloaded in Murmansk. Any questions?'

'A torpedo specialist?' asked Shushkin.

'I'll leave you to draw your own conclusions.'

MI5 HQ, 12.30pm

Sir Stephen Sharp and 'C', Sir Charles Lazenby-Smith, met on a regular basis. An update on Operation HENGIST, their joint plan to thwart the supply of Soviet SA-7 surface-to-air missiles to the Provisional IRA, was usually high on the agenda. In the late 1970s, two Vickers Viscount airliners operated by Air Rhodesia were shot down by insurgents equipped with these man-portable, shoulder-launched weapons. The loss of life had been considerable, but was confined to the passengers and crew onboard the aircraft. Bringing down a jumbo jet near Heathrow – or over central London – would be the ultimate 'spectacular'. London's emergency services had already practised for this nightmare scenario, assuming casualty figures in the thousands.

ETA, the Basque separatist group, was another interested party. SIS had uncovered close cooperation between ETA and the Provisionals. Denying them access to SA-7s – which had been supplied to countries and organisations within the Soviet sphere of influence – was of critical importance.

'C' had gone to Oxford rather than Cambridge, and, apart from being fluent in Russian and a short-service commission in the Guards, he seemed to have little in common with Sir Stephen. A confirmed batchelor, he loved opera and was a regular at the Royal Opera House, Covent Garden. He had not missed a Glyndebourne Festival for 20 years. To his coterie of friends he was always good company, quite the bon viveur, in fact. Now 48, the women on his arm tended to be somewhat younger and to have fallen on hard times of the emotional kind. He was quite open about working at the Foreign Office, though no one suspected the kind of 'overseas aid' he was actually connected with.

Their working lunch was in the cafeteria-style restaurant at MI5. The tables, with yellow formica tops and attendant Windsor-style chairs, were standard Civil Service issue, all made in England. All of the crockery came from The Potteries. The cutlery was made in Sheffield. The walls were painted white, though the shade was suitably soft. They were decorated with landscape prints from artists such as Constable, Gainsborough and Turner. According to Sir Stephen, the kitchen produced 'the best school meals in London'. The chef in charge was ex-Catering Corps, and the menu was varied though reassuringly traditional.

'You don't mind if Adrian joins us?'

'Not in the least,' said 'C'.

Fish and chips were a fixture on Fridays, which is what Sir Stephen selected. 'C', however, insisted on ordering something that was not on the menu – a ham and mushroom omelette with a green salad. This had happened before, and chef was more than up to the task. 'We've always got eggs, sir,' was his response when Sir Stephen went to apologise for a previous imposition.

After about three minutes the omelette was brought over to their table by one of the kitchen staff.

'Thank you so much,' said 'C'. His hosts were ready to tuck in.

'One of the things I enjoy about eating here,' said Sir Stephen, 'is not having to worry about how much butter I put on my bread. When I do this at home, Felicity looks at me as though I've turned into Jack the Ripper. I know her heart's in the right place, but –'

'She wants to make sure yours keeps on ticking,' said Boxted, who was content with some oxtail soup and a roll.

'This omelette really is excellent,' said 'C'.

'And one can't make one without a knob of butter,' said Sir Stephen, adding some more tartare sauce to his plate. 'I'm glad you're enjoying it... now put us in the picture, would you?'

'It all started with a certain advertising agency. It was set-up by a Colonel Blimp who used his gratuity – not to mention a sizable loan – to get the show on the road. Six months' in and the poor chap was losing money hand over fist – air-conditioned offices in Berkeley Square aren't exactly cheap. Just before the wheels were about to fly off, someone told me the whole sad story. So I went to see the Colonel, posing as a potential investor initially. He told me that he didn't have enough money to tempt a top director away from the big boys. All it took was a mere one-hundred and fifty thousand pounds.

He got his top director, and the TV money soon followed. In no time at all he had two or three premium clients. Trebles all round. Perhaps I've missed my true vocation?'

'I'm glad you can afford such largesse,' said Sir Stephen. 'I trust you're not on the board of directors?'

'Let's just say I'm a sleeping partner. SJ Associates trades normally, and the loan is being repaid at slightly below market rates – less the retainer Johnson receives for his services. His company is the nexus of our Spanish operation, hidden – if not on the plain – then certainly in plain sight.'

'And Zoborski?'

'On her last visit to Canada in July, Nineteen Eighty-One, she was approached by the KGB in Calgary. They explained that her father had outlived his usefulness, and that he might not enjoy a long and happy retirement unless she was prepared to be recruited. Sophie played for time, said she was being asked to make an impossible choice – then got in touch with our embassy in Ottawa. We briefed her on how to play the next meeting. Moscow Centre think they have a sleeper – a mutually beneficial arrangement. Evidently they intend saving her for something big.'

'And in the meantime, she's been working for you?'

'She was too good to miss – no pun intended.'

'Are you absolutely sure about her?'

'C' gave Sir Stephen a wry smile. 'Dangled in front of us, you mean? I can assure you we vetted her thoroughly. As you know, she served in the Rhine Army, and we looked for anything that might have blotted her copybook. The only thing that came up was her father – and you know all about that. I myself briefed her on his true identity. She was as steady as a rock.'

'So there's not a scintilla of doubt?'

'I wouldn't have asked the Brigadier to release her from the Corps otherwise. The date we agreed upon ensured she didn't lose her Long Service and Good Conduct Medal.'

'And you didn't feel the need to share any of this with me?'

'I thought it best to keep her hermetically sealed. It's not as if I've been holding back on HENGIST – you have everything you need.'

116

'For which I'm eternally grateful. But had I known she was onside…'

'I know – you could have made your dispositions accordingly. Are you going to order dessert?'

'I'd rather hear more about Zoborski first.'

'As you know, I don't like to stint myself where pudding is concerned.'

'I do indeed,' said Sir Stephen, raising an admonishing eyebrow. 'I think you'll find the fruit salad is rather good. I usually have a scoop of vanilla ice cream with mine.'

'I think I'll have the treacle tart with custard,' said 'C'.

'Now, about Zoborski…'

'She spent a week or two in Washington before coming back to the UK. I was in town at the time, and we met in the embassy. She'd agreed to swim for the inter-services team – "Coming out of retirement" was how she put it – in a friendly against the combined US forces. She won all of her events, which was quite remarkable considering the average age of the opposition seemed to be about twenty-two.'

'Quite the little mermaid, I hear?'

'And whip-smart with it. Later on she went for a swim in the Pentagon at the personal invitation of Gene Bullett, one of the admirals on their planning staff. He also invited her to a cocktail party at this house.'

'A purely social interaction?'

'She told me he was quite attentive, and soon found out his wife had departed for pastures new. He certainly had some wind in his sails, but that's about as far as it went.'

'What brought you to Washington?'

'The CIA thought they were on to a mole, namely Manfred Lorenz, the West German defence attaché They weren't sure who was running him – the KGB or Anton. ('Anton' was the shorthand used by 'C' for East Germany's foreign intelligence service: Main Directorate A.) They allowed him privileged access to the Pentagon, and began to staircase him through the various levels. – until he thought he'd got to the general in charge of updating the target list

117

for NATO's tactical nuclear weapons, something of irresistible interest.'

'Did he take the bait?'

'Up to the elbow. He went double for them, though unlike Sophie I *did* have my doubts. I said as much when Langley asked me for a second opinion.'

'So when did Zoborski enter the fray?'

'Last summer, in San Sebastian. The girl I'd originally assigned simply wasn't up to it – she'd had a narrow squeak in East Berlin and her nerves were shredded. So I brought Sophie in. Her task was to gain intelligence on what ETA were doing vis-a-vis arms shipments in general and SA-7s in particular. She became part of the team operating in the Basque country.

'She posed – in every sense – as a tourist seeking solace after a recent divorce. She attracted plenty of admirers on La Concha Beach, and one of them was already a subject of interest. If anything, not having much Spanish helped maintain her cover. She was able to plant devices in cars and at least one meeting place used by the group. After three weeks I felt it was time to bring her back, before her plausibility began to pale. That was just over a month ago.'

'Hence the rich seam of new information.'

'We sent CNI edited transcripts of the key recordings. She was back in Berkeley Square when Segev bumped into her. We already knew that Mossad were targeting Arnold. Once he'd crossed their path his fate was sealed – it just so happened that the Guarda Civil beat them to it.'

'Why did Zoborski get involved?'

'We needed someone to contact Logaris. She knew all about Arnold's ambition to become a merchant of death. Berkowitz was expected to share that intelligence, and, when he didn't, she did – with her CIA handler. Langley had serious concerns about Berkowitz's politics and his methods – concerns that turned out to be well-founded.'

'What did she have?'

'The file on his unofficial operations. It was in a microdot hidden in one of the buttons she gave to Zoborski, which we then recovered from her car at Fairoaks. In return for exit visas for two Jewish

118

nuclear scientists, Berkowitz was prepared to cooperate with Moscow Centre in some tightly defined areas, chiefly disinformation and, to a limited extent, counter-espionage.'

'Was yesterday's attack some kind of twisted revenge – has Logaris been compromised?'

'There's no sign of that – there has to be something else, something in the deep background...'

'How was your tart?'

'Absolutely first class.'

'Cheese and biscuits?'

'Just a small coffee, thank you. I've had an elegant sufficiency.'

RAF Methbridge,Suffolk, 2.35pm

Major Rico Hamlee, a USAF exchange officer, was using his putting improver to pass the time on 'Q', otherwise known as QRA: Quick Reaction Alert. His navigator, Pilot Officer Brian Hopkins, was deep in the May issue of *What Car?* magazine, studying the relative merits of the turbocharged Colt Mirage, MG Metro and Renault 5. He was ready to trade-in the Mark 1 Escort van given to him by his father, a self-employed electrician in Basingstoke.

Hamlee's handicap was in single figures. He'd been delighted to discover the RAF had several golf courses, all of which he intended to play before his exchange posting was over. Tall and lanky, he sported an impeccably trimmed moustache. His light brown hair was cut short, astronaut-style. At 39, he was the archetypal, steely-eye, fighter pilot. He'd crewed up with Hopkins on the firm recommendation of the station commander.

His wife, Suzy, 36, was a gorgeous California blonde who taught aerobics at the station gym in addition to looking after their son, 14-year-old Rico Jr. Their roots were in Sacramento, capital of the 'Golden State'.

They had slotted easily into the social scene at the station. When, at a recent fancy dress party at the officers' mess, Suzy went as 'Sandy' from the 1978 movie 'Grease' – complete with teased hair and spandex – jaws had gone into freefall.

Hopkins, at twenty-two, was a first-tourist on the squadron. He was comfortably under six foot, with a fine head of dark brown hair parted at the side. He didn't like having it cut, and had his own, rather liberal interpretation of the relevant Queen's Regulations. Fortunately this fitted in with the policy of making off-duty service personnel less conspicuous to IRA units on the UK mainland. Though he claimed not to be a fitness fanatic, he could beat anyone on the station at squash, his favourite game by far. He certainly seemed to know all the angles, and there was no doubting his brilliance with radar – he had passed top of his course at the Phantom OCU (Operational Conversion Unit).

The jet assigned to them, a Phantom FGR.2, serial number XV547, code letter 'B' for Bravo, was not exactly new. It had come off the line in 1968 at the St Louis, Missouri, plant of the McDonnell Douglas Corporation. The RAF had followed the Royal Navy in ordering the F-4 Phantom. Why buy American? Simple – all rival British contenders had been cancelled by a government which, depending on where your loyalties were, was either knocking heads together for the greater good, or doing its best to cripple a once-great industry. Sourcing a significant proportion of the Phantom's all-important avionics and associated equipment from UK companies did, however, help to cut the ground from beneath the feet of the government's more embittered critics.

The biggest change was the substitution of Rolls-Royce Spey engines for the General Electric J79 units fitted to the standard aircraft. The switch to the Spey proved the Derby firm had political power, too – they made it quite clear that denuding their factories of military engine work would be totally unacceptable. The Spey matured into a fine engine, but it was bigger and heavier than the well-proven J79, and the resulting higher drag and weight penalties cancelled out the extra poke.

Hamlee was more familiar with the all-American F-4E, which he had first flown in 1969. This version came with some major upgrades that were introduced as a result of bitter combat experience in Vietnam. Perhaps the most important change was the introduction of an internal 20 millimetre six-barrel M61 rotary cannon, which was fitted under the radar in the nose. Many MiGs had escaped when a Phantom had been too close to use its Sidewinder missiles – or had simply used them all up. RAF Phantoms could be equipped with the same weapon, but it had to be carried in a gun pod under the centreline. With the UK Air Defence Region covering about one million square miles, the Phantoms allocated to QRA needed as much fuel as they could carry. So although the M61 could fire up to 100 high-explosive rounds per second, it was left on the ground in favour of a large external fuel tank.

As the flying qualities of all Phantoms were essentially the same, Hamlee's transition to the RAF version was fairly straightforward. The Phantom was undoubtedly a popular aircraft – but it could bite an unwary pilot hard. Unlike the F-16 – designed with computerised fly-by-wire controls which prevented the pilot from inadvertently overstressing or mishandling the aircraft – the Phantom had some dark and dangerous corners in its flight envelope. These included a marked reluctance to obey normal control inputs when manoeuvring at high angles of attack (in other words, when the jet was flying in a different direction to where its nose was pointing). Problems typically occurred in an adrenaline-fuelled dogfight. The Phantom lacked the sparkling agility of the F-16, and, if a pilot tried to push the limits too far, the aircraft would depart from controlled flight – and sometimes there was simply not enough time or altitude for recovery. That meant ejecting – and not everyone pulled the handle in time.

Where the Phantom excelled was in engaging targets at beyond visual range (BVR). Hence the highly trained navigator sat behind the pilot in a separate cockpit. Being less traditional than the RAF, the USAF preferred to call them Weapon Systems Officers – 'whizzos' for short. Their primary job was to manipulate the powerful Westinghouse AN/AWG-12 radar. Importantly, this was of the pulse-Doppler type, which enabled a good operator like Hopkins to pick up a distant target at high- or low-level. He would then guide the pilot into the optimum position for missile launch. In peacetime, that invariably meant practice interceptions (PIs), though the skill involved kept every crew primed for the real thing.

As Hamlee completed another putt, Hopkins decided to confide in him. 'I've been thinking about applying for pilot training.'

'Go for it – any dumb-ass can fly a jet. The tricky bit is operating the weapon system, and you can certainly do that.'

Hamlee was, at best, only half-right. Only a small percentage in any given population have the mental equipment and aptitude to make the grade, either for the military or the airlines. Fighter pilots are even more special – they have to keep sensory and mental overload at bay in a deadly game of three-dimensional chess. And although there are some basic rules to follow, every combat tends to be different. Generally speaking, the first pilot to make a mistake is the one that doesn't go home...

The Antonov followed the central air corridor from West Berlin. It was one of three established by mutual agreement between the Western Allies and the Soviet Union at the end of World War 2. Each corridor was 20 miles (32 kilometres) wide, and their integrity was strictly enforced. Koslov cross-checked the autopilot as they maintained a steady course, while Shushkin helped with the lookout and monitored the radio. The weather was good, and after two hours' steady progress they could see the south coast of England emerging from under a layer of low cloud. The flight was proceeding normally, exactly on schedule.

In London it was a pleasant, sunny, Friday afternoon. Boxted was already ready looking forward to taking his Campervan to the South Downs for the weekend. Sir Stephen was planning a cruise on the Thames in *Serenade*. The bad news arrived at just after 3.25pm. They were enjoying some refreshments from the hostess trolley sent up by the canteen. Sir Stephen was just biting into a slice of his favourite fruitcake when there was a knock at the door. Boxted answered on his behalf: 'Come!'

Mary came through with a signal. It was marked MOST IMMEDIATE. Sir Stephen calmly took a sip of tea, though he didn't return the cup to its saucer until he had read the entire message. 'Acknowledge it, would you?' She nodded, turned and closed the door behind her.

'Where's Spinney Heath airfield, Adrian?'

'Bedfordshire. I believe it's used for test flying by the MoD.'

'There's been a break-in. A new type of torpedo has gone missing. Apparently it has a rather special warhead.'

'Not –'

'No, not nuclear, thank god – though fifty kilograms of Torpex is hardly trivial.'

'I'll call Gibson. He's at West Midlands Airport.'

'You mean there's another one of those cargo flights today?'

'Absolutely.'

'It must be stopped. Tell him to use any pretext.'

Gibson was also enjoying a cuppa when he was beckoned to the phone. 'There isn't much time, Gibbo. Has that Russian aircraft taken off yet?'

'Yes – it departed right on time a few minutes ago, at fifteen thirty hours.'

'Damn!'

'What's wrong?'

'We seem to be missing a rather special torpedo.'

'Take it from me – there's nothing remotely that size on board. I watched it in and I watched it out again. They did have more duty free with them this time, though.'

'Then they must be landing somewhere else. Have a word with air traffic – let me know if they spot anything. I'll get on to Strike Command.'

Gibson found the duty controller, who had seen the aircraft briefly on primary radar before it descended towards Cullingthorpe. The loss of both radio and radar contact was duly reported. After taking a call from Gibson, Boxsted was back on the phone to the air officer commander-in-chief (AOC-in-C), who now thought it prudent to inform the cabinet office at 10 Downing Street. Within minutes he was appraising the cabinet secretary about what the Antonov was probably up to. As a result the senior fighter controller at a radar station in Norfolk had received orders to intercept the aircraft and, if necessary, prevent it from leaving sovereign UK airspace.

Hamlee was having a power nap when Corporal Keswick, a drill instructor from the RAF Regiment, called in unexpectedly. 'Sorry to disturb you, Major – how's your sword drill these days?'

'Sword drill?'

'The Station Commander sends his compliments. He's unavailable for the AOC's inspection next Tuesday. As you carry the rank, he wondered if you would like to take the parade?'

Hopkins was smiling. 'Taking it out is easy… the difficult bit is putting it back in again.'

Any further comment on the subject was interrupted by the phone. Hopkins picked up. His smile disappeared rather quickly.

'Is it for me?' asked Hamlee.

Hopkins' hand flew up into a stop signal. He needed to listen. 'I see... of course, sir... we'll be ready.'

Sword drill was now the last thing on their minds. 'That was the AOC himself. A Russian cargo plane has gone missing after taking off from West Midlands Airport. We're to go as we are, there's –'

The squawk box crackled into life: 'Southern QRA... vector Three Two Zero, low-level, call Kestrel Control on stud two-three, backup two-seven, mission Alpha Zero One, SCRAMBLE, SCRAMBLE, SCRAMBLE. Acknowledge.'

Hamlee jabbed the transmit switch and duly acknowledged the order to scramble with a curt 'Q'. As they dashed out to the jet, the warning Klaxon was blaring like a demented Dalek. This was no exercise – this one was going all the way.

Their Phantom, 26 tons of latent malevolence, towered above them. Plugged in to the external electrical power provided by a diesel-fuelled Houchin starter pack, it was already coming alive. Detachable ladders that might have been made with offcuts from the Forth Bridge gave access to each cockpit. Hamlee's flying helmet was parked on the canopy hoop, from where he could easily pull it down and roll it over his head. Hopkins preferred to don his helmet and Mae West at the bottom of the ladder. Every crew was different, and made their own individual arrangements. What counted was speed. After thirty seconds both men were strapped into their parachutes and ejection seats. Their well-drilled ground crew, as slick as any in Formula One, were busy readying the jet for immediate launch.

A brisk twirl from Hamlee's index finger indicated he was ready to start. He selected engine master switches ON. The Houchin took the load. Left engine start switch ON. Right engine start switch ON. The rest of the starting sequence was automatic. The revolutions on both engines increased as Hamlee monitored the fire warning lights, turbine gas temperature (TGT), nozzles, fuel flows, oil pressure and numerous other items on the checklist. From left to right, he quickly scanned the gauges, switches and controls – all good. As they waited for the inertial navigation system to align correctly, the noise inside the hardened aircraft shelter (HAS) rose from the merely deafening to the apocalyptic.

It was time to go. The access ladders were pulled away, and Hamlee's waving hands were the signal to disconnect the Houchin, arm the medium-range Sky Flash missiles, whip the protective nose caps off the short-range Sidewinders and remove the wheel chocks. He gave the marshaller a snappy salute as the jet emerged from the shed and turned straight on to the high speed taxiway. More checks, challenge-and-response style, went back and forth. Some are more obvious than others. The one to unfold and lock the outer wings – a reminder the Phantom was designed for the confines of a carrier deck – should be hard to miss. But not impossible: more than one jet had managed to take off with its wings still folded...

Time to double-check their ejection seat safety pins (fourteen in total) were stowed. Hamlee's new gloves were not quite snug enough, so he pulled them on tighter, making a fist with each hand in turn, then locked his fingers together a few times. Satisfied, he selected half flap, which would not only reduce the run but also make the jet more controllable at lift off.

There was no holding short or stopping to line up with the runway. Take off began on the roll straight from the taxiway. Just under three minutes from the call to scramble, Hamlee's left hand pushed the throttles smartly up to the first stop – full Military power. His next action was the one the little group of plane spotters gathered at the boundary fence were waiting for. He rocked the throttles up into full afterburner. Even in daylight the shock diamonds shooting back from the jetpipes – indicating supersonic flow – were clearly visible. Fuel was being consumed at nearly 2,000 pounds per minute, but the extra thrust accelerated them to unstick in around 15 seconds. At 180 knots, Hamlee selected the gear and flaps up, then stayed low to build energy. He waited until he had 300 knots before making a steep right turn. Only when he'd rolled out on heading did the afterburners fade, the spotters following the Phantom's smoky trail until it was out of sight. They listened as the tidal wave of decibels became a dissonant rumble, dissipating across the landscape.

The weather is supposed to be neutral – even in a Cold War – though that was far from the case as the Antonov began its descent into Cullingthorpe. The 'isolated showers' had suddenly become a lot less isolated. A cluster of heavy rain clouds, like dark grey sponges, were busy unloading tons of water on the airfield. The windscreen wipers snipped stoically against the deluge, but it was like trying to see through glass-bottle lenses. The runway was out there... somewhere.

Most airports have an ILS (instrument landing system) which, once captured, gives pilots precise vertical and lateral guidance to the runway. This is extremely useful in conditions of poor visibility. Being able to find the runway is a prerequisite for landing on it. Of necessity the approach to Cullingthorpe had to be entirely visual – except right now it wasn't.

'Do you have it?' asked Koslov.

'No,' replied Shushkin, 'I can't see anything!'

Though he had configured the aircraft to maintain a steady three-degree glideslope, he was effectively flying blind. They were on a good heading for the runway – 240 degrees – but with no precise height indication they were in danger of flying into the ground.

'We'll have to go-around,' said Koslov, pushing the power levers forward. Within seconds they had flown out of the downpour into clear air. The runway had been dead ahead – but they were now halfway along it and flying at 200 metres – too late to make a landing. If Koslov was frustrated, he didn't show it. Instead he hauled them into the tightest possible left turn, reducing power as they curved back towards the runway. Shushkin was watching a master at work.

With the left wingtip barely fifty metres above the ground, he straightened up bang on centreline. The actual landing was more splashdown than touchdown. After a ground roll of 1,800 metres, they had slowed to a fast walking pace, at which point Koslov switched to nosewheel steering and made a 180 degree turn to backtrack along the runway. A long wheel base Land Rover was waiting at the threshold. It was a dark green Series II, with the headlamps in the front grille panel.

'Take over,' said Koslov. 'Be ready to roll as soon as I get back.'

The men in the Land Rover helped to guide the container as it was winched deep inside the cargo hold. Belyakov was about to walk back from the edge of the ramp when he saw Malenkovich sprinting away to his left, heading for a small wood on the airfield boundary. He jumped off, and was soon running him down. When he had closed to within about twenty metres he shouted a clear warning: 'Stop – or I shoot!'

Malenkovich looked back, losing his footing in the process. He fell, then scrambled back to his feet and carried on running. Belyakov drew a concealed Makarov PB automatic – he didn't need to bother with the suppressor. He squeezed the trigger at least four times, but the shots could hardly be heard above the din from the engines.

Malenkovich fell again – but this time he didn't get up. He'd been hit squarely between the shoulder blades. His revolutionary zeal had only been a front. He'd wanted to make a move at the airport, but, after catching the eye of Belyakov, his nerve had failed. The temptation to make a run for it while everyone was preoccupied with the loading operation had proved irresistible, however. He'd opened the access door below the left wing root, and might well have slipped away had he had the presence of mind to run in a different direction. Now he was dead, lying face down like a discarded mannequin.

By now the Antonov should have been on its way. More precious seconds had ticked by as Belyakov dashed back on board.

'Was that really necessary?' said Koslov.

'No defectors – those were my orders.'

Retrieving the body was out of the question. They had been on the ground for nearly three minutes, twice as long as originally planned. At least the weather had improved – the skies were now clear.

'Close the cargo doors!' ordered Koslov as he dashed back to the cockpit. Shushkin's right hand was already pushing the power levers forward to the stops. A combined 16,000 shaft horsepower, converted into thrust by sixteen propeller blades, was sending spirals of vapour back across the wings.

The standing water they had plunged into on landing again checked their speed. Twenty seconds after brake release all ten tyres were still firmly on the runway. As the spray billowed up and over the wings, the lumbering Antonov looked more like a flying boat than a land plane. Shushkin became fixated on the jagged web of discarded farm implements looming ahead. With less than 500 metres remaining, they were back on dry concrete. It was too late to even think about aborting the take-off. They were committed.

Koslov took over: 'I've got her.' Just as it seemed certain they were going to be sliced up and become a fireball of fuel and twisted metal, he pulled back firmly on the yoke. They lifted cleanly into the air, climbing strongly. Twenty metres... fifty metres...

'Gear up.' The relief in Koslov's voice was shared by Shushkin, who had moved the lever on the 'g' of 'gear'. As he began to bring up the flaps, Koslov levelled off at barely one hundred metres. Sitev was scanning his instrument panel for any abnormal indications. He need not have worried. Everything was in the green – the engines were operating perfectly.

As the village of Cullingthorpe receded into the distance, Pavlovich maintained a sharp lookout from the tail turret, which lacked the twin 23 millimetre cannon fitted to military versions of the An-12. Yakovlev took up position in the glazed nose, where he could concentrate on navigating visually. It was vital to stay on track and reach the coast as quickly as possible. After skirting Gibraltar Point it would take less than three minutes to reach the protection of international airspace.

'We can start breathing again,' said Koslov.

'I'm still thinking about that take-off,' replied Shushkin.

'Let's hope we haven't used up all our luck…'

'Alpha Zero One, this is Kestrel Control. Steer Three Three Zero, last known contact ten miles east of West Midlands Airport.' It was a bright, female voice cutting through the static. 'You are cleared high speed.'

Hamlee acknowledged: 'Roger, Zero One.'

Hopkins was operating the radar system with his usual calm assurance. A target flying at low-level is the most difficult to acquire, both visually and on radar – finding the Antonov was far from being a foregone conclusion. Ground clutter from terrain and buildings – even road traffic – had to be filtered out. 'I need more height, Rico.'

Hamlee added a touch of back pressure on the control stick and they climbed rapidly from 2,000 to 10,000 feet. On the way they punched through a line of small cumulus clouds, outriders of the towering cumulonimbus that had developed during the afternoon. The grandeur of the cloudscape, and occasional flashes of lightning, were blotted out as they worked as a team to find their quarry. The radar was now in 'look down' mode, and flying higher made Hopkins' task much easier. They were bang on track, speed Mach 0.85 with 55 nautical miles to run, a distance they would eat up in a little under seven minutes.

'I've got a contact,' announced Hopkins. 'Ten right at eleven miles. Steer Three Five Zero.'

He was setting up a classic curve of pursuit, which would bring them in behind the Antonov, from the south-west.

Pavlovich was enjoying a panoramic view of the Norfolk countryside as it raced away beneath him. Broad fields, anchored by farm houses and hamlets, moved towards the horizon as if on a giant conveyor belt. The smoky trails left by the engines were ruler-straight until small air currents cut them into swirly, ribbon-like segments. Then another smoky trail appeared, ahead of which was a dark shape, as yet indistinct. When it reappeared after flying through a layer of low cloud, Pavlovich swallowed hard. 'English Phantom!' he announced over the intercom.

'Where?' asked Koslov.

'He's overtaking us on our left... I've lost sight of him now.'

'Don't worry, I've got him.'

The Phantom was busy giving his Antonov the once-over. Hopkins jotted down the registration on his kneeboard: CCCP-07119. They had never even seen a 'Cub' – its NATO reporting name – before. It was flying barely 100 feet above the ground at 270 knots. Hamlee checked in with Kestrel Control: 'Alpha Zero One...

we've intercepted a Cub aircraft... heading Zero Six Zero, at extremely low level... he's nap-of-the-earth.'

'Thank you, Alpha Zero One.'

'The aircraft appears to be civilian... no visible armament.'

'Alpha Zero One, escort it to the nearest suitable airfield. Norwich is available.'

'Roger.'

Hamlee nudged the throttles forward and moved into a position on the left and slightly ahead of the Antonov. Next came some gentle wing rocking and flashing of navigation nights, the internationally agreed signals for 'you have been intercepted – follow me'. Koslov should have acknowledged in kind and climbed to a safer altitude. Instead he simply ignored them.

Hamlee now moved into even tighter formation – close enough to make eye contact with Koslov. He changed hands on the stick and stabbed his index finger downwards. The last time he had intercepted a Soviet aircraft it had been a 'Bear Delta' long range bomber, cruising serenely past the north coast of Iceland at 26,000 feet. Its crew had waved at him from behind every transparency, and he had waved back. But not this time. Today was different.

Hopkins felt distinctly uneasy about the proximity of the two aircraft. Staying close enough to swap paint demanded total concentration. Hamlee hadn't seen the line of electricity pylons marching across their path. Koslov saw them, but very late, and pulled up to clear the top of the nearest pylon. The first Hopkins knew about it was the instant onset of heavy G forces as Hamlee reacted – they only just avoided the wires.

'Alpha Zero One, any response from the Cub?' Hamlee didn't reply with his customary rapidity. 'Alpha Zero One, acknowledge...'

'Sorry guys, I've been kinda busy. No change in speed or heading... looks like he's getting outta Dodge.'

There was a long pause. Then, a deeper, male voice: 'This is the senior fighter controller. As soon as the target is over the sea you are cleared to engage. I repeat – you are cleared to engage.'

'You want me to splash him?'

'Affirmative. This concerns the Defence of the Realm. Check switchcs live.'

'What is this?' said Hamlee, speaking to Hopkins on the intercom, 'King Arthur and the knights of the round table?'

'He nearly wiped us out back there.'

'Yeah... that was a close one. Are you okay?'

'I'm fine. We're running out of time, Rico.'

'Alpha Zero One, acknowledge...'

'He's just gone feet wet over The Wash, still on heading Zero Six Zero. We're engaging. Alpha Zero One.'

Hamlee reduced power and slipped smoothly behind the Antonov. He moved the Master Arm Switch (MAS) from SAFE to ARM, then checked his weapon status panel. 'All good in back?' Hopkins glanced by his right knee to check the relevant circuit breaker was in place. 'Affirmative.' Their Phantom was now combat ready.

Koslov was only too well aware of the danger: 'I noticed he didn't have a gun when he came in close – otherwise we'd be confetti by now. So that means he'll be lining up a missile.'

'But we are defenceless,' said Shushkin, anxiously. 'We have no countermeasures.'

'How far now, Yakovlev?'

'Sixteen kilometres to go, Colonel. Just under two minutes.'

'We might have a chance,' said Koslov. 'Just keep those power levers all the way forward.'

'We're already at max power,' replied Shushkin. 'And I'm pushing as hard as I can!'

Hamlee was indeed setting up his Sidewinders. Four lights, each captioned SWR on the missile status panel, confirmed they were now available. Importantly, he'd made sure coolant was selected ON. This had to be done at least one minute before firing, otherwise the missile's sensitive infrared seeker would be unable to detect and track the target.

The Sidewinder was by far the most successful air-to-air missile in service anywhere in the world. The AIM-9G or 'Golf' model which armed their Phantom was not as advanced as the latest AIM-9L, the deadly 'Lima' which had given the Royal Navy's Sea Harriers such a decisive edge against Argentine combat aircraft the year before in the South Atlantic. Unlike the Lima, which could be launched from virtually any direction (including head-on), even

131

against a 'non-cooperative' (ie, manoeuvring) target, the Golf had less generous regions of launch acceptability. That meant they had to position their Phantom behind the Antonov, ideally with the smallest angle from dead astern (six o'clock) as possible.

The Phantom was now about two miles behind its quarry, slightly higher at seven o'clock. Hamlee was expecting to hear a 'growling' tone in his headset – indicating the target was inside the missile's launch envelope. But the Antonov was so low it was almost merging with the sea. When the growl did come, it kept modulating as the Sidewinder hunted for the Antonov's exhaust plumes.

Hamlee wasn't happy: 'I'm not getting good tone, goddammit!' Then, momentarily, the growl became stronger, steadier. He squeezed the trigger, calling out the NATO code used when firing an infrared-guided missile: 'Fox Two.'

With Pavlovich keeping a sharp lookout from the rear turret, Koslov was able to anticipate their attack, and had already begun to haul back on the yoke with all his strength. His climbing turn towards the Phantom increased the rate of closure and angle-off simultaneously. Importantly, it also began to point the hot exhaust from his engines away from the Sidewinder's infrared seeker. Koslov was thinking like a fighter pilot – but his timing still had to be nigh on perfect.

Pavlovich saw the burst of flame and smoke: 'Missile!'

The Sidewinder had accelerated to Mach 2 in as many seconds. Yet time now seemed to elongate... Hamlee had fired at close to minimum range, and the safety factors built-in to ensure the missile did not threaten his Phantom now acted against him – it did not go 'active' soon enough. So his Sidewinder fell away like a spent arrow. The angle off had become too extreme – his missile had failed to 'cut the corner'.

Hamlee could hardly believe it: 'Shit!'

'What went wrong?' asked Hopkins.

'There must be one helluva good stick in that cockpit.'

Pavlovich was equally impressed: 'That was a brilliant manoeuvre, Colonel!'

'You're now my rear-warning radar. Try not to lose him.'

'I won't... you can depend on me, Colonel!'

132

As the Phantom passed overhead, Koslov reversed course, all the while descending until they were barely above the waves.

If the Antonov was ill-suited for this kind of manoeuvring, the Phantom was also well outside its comfort zone. Designed as a 'shoot and scoot' weapons system, it had often struggled against the more nimble MiGs encountered over Vietnam. Hamlee had been there – and not being allowed to use the Phantom's BVR capability had cost him, he believed, two certain kills. The rules of engagement demanded a positive visual identification before any missiles were fired. Washington did not want any 'blue on blue' kills.

He couldn't have gone BVR against Koslov, either. Apart from the serious matter of disregarding international law, it would have meant putting civilian lives and property at risk, both from stray missiles or from the Antonov hitting the ground.

They were duelling the old-fashioned way, with stick and rudder. Koslov had to be careful not to overstress the Antonov, though its purely manual controls had a built-in safety factor – they firmed up like setting concrete. It required a fair amount of muscle power to make the aircraft turn at all. In contrast, the Phantom had power-boosted controls and could generally manoeuvre with only small movements on the stick. The down side was that manoeuvring at a safe speed took up a lot of sky. Getting low and slow risked losing control. Hamlee decided it was time to get leaner and meaner. 'I'm punching off the tanks.'

Pavlovich saw the centreline and two underwing drop tanks tumble into the sea, and reported this to Koslov. Once again, as Hamlee tried to set up a shot, Koslov turned back into him as aggressively as he could before resuming a north-easterly heading. He was flying a racetrack pattern, inexorably gaining on the invisible line that marked the beginning of international airspace – and sanctuary from any further attacks. Even the prevailing south-westerly wind was in their favour.

But flying this low over the sea was unhealthy. Any significant contact – such as touching a wing tip – would be catastrophic. Koslov could see 500 kilometres per hour on his airspeed indicator, which meant they were travelling at nearly 139 metres per second. The slightest miscalculation would turn them all into fish food. So when Koslov saw an exploration rig under tow dead ahead he had no choice but to climb – and that made them vulnerable.

Rather than trying to reel the target in again, Hamlee decided to let his fish run away with the line. Out popped the speedbrakes, back came the throttles, down went the flaps, until the jet stabilised at 250 knots. Aware that his opposite number had a second pair of eyes, he turned away from the massive legs of the rig and stayed ultra low – both for concealment and to give his next missile a better look at its prey. 'How long before he's outside, Brian?'

'Thirty-five seconds.'

Koslov knew the Phantom was still out there, stalking him. 'Where is he now, Pavlovich.'

'I... I've lost him!'

Half a mile away at ten o'clock, the Antonov stood out like a giant white gull. In contrast, the Phantom's tactical camouflage made it extremely difficult to spot. Hopkins could feel the aircraft twitch as it flattened out little pockets of air thrown up by the waves. When he looked outside the sea was glossy grey, like paint. Normally he'd have given a 'check height' warning long before now. Instead he continued the countdown: 'Twenty seconds...'

It was time to throw the throttles forward. Hamlee checked back on the stick and banked hard left. Up came the flaps as the Phantom howled in full afterburner. The G forces piled in... 3,4,5... until he unloaded and smoothly brought the sight onto the target.

'Ten seconds...'

The pipper was dead centre. The growl in his headset had never been stronger. The angle off was barely five degrees. There was no need to sweeten the shot. It was a perfect set up. He squeezed the trigger a second time...

Pavlovich, nervously quartering sea and sky, finally eyeballed the Phantom as it came in for the kill. 'Right, seven o'clock low – MISSILE!' Koslov's flying had been epic, but the one-sided battle was nearly over.

The Sidewinder shimmied lazily in the terminal phase. It was a little dance of death. The ice cold eye of its infrared seeker remained locked on target. A split second later its electronic brain activated the proximity fuse. Propelled by high explosive, a lethal ring of steel expanded into the sky.

Shushkin ducked instinctively as hot metal clattered into the right wing. The outboard engine immediately went into a kind of mechanical spasm, its revolutions fluctuating wildly. 'Secure Number Four,' said Koslov, calmly.

The flight engineer, Sitev, didn't need a checklist – he had practised the drills a thousand times. As the engine powered down, Shushkin could see chunks missing from the propeller blades and numerous puncture marks under the wing. Worse, an intense fire was sending sparks back through the exhaust. Sitev, already busy transferring fuel from the damaged tanks, saw the fire warning light illuminate. He wasted no time in pressing the extinguisher button on his control panel.

There were no celebratory whoops from the Phantom's cockpit. They could see a stream of white smoke trailing back from the stricken engine.

'Son of a bitch...'

Hamlee's under-the-breath remark was far from being an insult – he was paying Koslov a compliment.

'Alpha Zero One... anything to report?'

'We've hit one of his engines... but he's still flying. It's too late for another shot.'

'Alpha Zero Two will take over, closing now from your five o'clock, same level.'

'Visual.'

The crew of the second Phantom had had time to put on their immersion suits – vital for survival should they happen to come down in the North Sea, let alone the arctic. They would now shadow the Cub from a respectful distance.

'Alpha Zero One, check switches safe and return to base.'

'That's a roger, Zero One.'

'All we have to worry about now is the debrief,' said Hopkins.

The crew of the Antonov had a lot more to worry about. 'We have another fire,' said Shushkin.

Flames were breaking through numerous holes in the wing – they would not be airborne for much longer. Koslov's next command was inevitable: 'Everyone – don your life jackets and prepare for ditching. As soon as we come to a stop, make your way to the forward bulkhead... we'll use the cockpit escape hatch.'

Shushkin kept his first thought to himself: *That sea doesn't look very inviting...*

'It's time to transmit a Mayday on the discrete frequency,' said Koslov. 'We have only a few minutes, maybe less.'

Shushkin's distress call was answered by the *Petrushka*, a Soviet AGI (Auxiliary, General Intelligence) vessel positioned for just such a contingency. She was a trawler of 690 tons – but had never caught any fish.

'*Petrushka* is making best speed towards our position. I'll get your life jacket, Artem Alexey.'

Koslov throttled back, then banked the Antonov gently to the left, all the while assessing the sea state. There was a moderate swell, and he was aiming to land between the swells in textbook fashion. He was working hard to keep the aircraft steady. His big fear was that the fire had weakened the main spar. If it failed the wing would fold up like paper.

Shushkin returned to his seat with their life jackets, which they put on in turn while the other had the controls.

'We'll try and touch tail first,' said Koslov. 'I don't want us turning into a submarine.'

The fire was destroying a significant amount of lift from the damaged wing, so they had to compensate by flying faster. Too slow and they would stall – and tumble into the sea. Koslov compromised with half flap, keeping plenty of speed and power in hand. The landing gear had to remain retracted, further increasing their approach speed. 'Time to raise the nose,' said Koslov. They started pulling... back, back – back – back –

There was a terrific jolt as the sea came up to meet them, followed by a succession of thuds and bangs as various panels gave way. After a brief flurry of spray from the propellers, the remaining engines spluttered and died. At least the fire was out.

In the silence that followed came one, overriding, realisation – they were already sinking. Koslov released his harness, opened up the overhead the escape hatch and shouted: 'Abandon aircraft!'

The dinghy was stowed at the front of the cargo compartment, and Yakovlev and Pavlovich managed to push it out the side door. The water was already at waist-level. By the time Koslov was ready to leave, most of the fuselage was awash. He was nearly outside when a big wave broke over the hatch, slapping him back down like a giant hand. Shushkin went back in to retrieve his friend. He managed to push him through the hatch with only seconds to spare.

'She's going,' said Yakovlev. Everyone stepped off, then kicked as hard as they could. Belyakov was the strongest swimmer. He was first to reach the dinghy, and pulled the toggle to inflate it. Their life jackets kept them afloat until, one by one, the others clambered aboard. It had been a struggle: the coldness of the sea had sapped their strength. Everyone needed to catch their second wind. They had drifted no more than twenty metres when the left wing began to rise and twist until it was almost vertical. Then it followed the rest of the aircraft down into the depths.

Koslov was bleeding from a head wound, and lapsing into unconsciousness. Belyakov took out his combat knife and cut away a sleeve from his tunic. His improvised bandage was better than nothing, but everyone was thinking the same thing: '*Petrushka* can't arrive soon enough.'

Alpha Zero Two reported the crash, and the duty controller alerted the RAF Search and Rescue Coordination Centre, which had scrambled a Sea King helicopter from a base on the East Coast. The first to hear the steady beat of its rotor blades was Yakovlev. He pointed towards the bright yellow shape in the distance.

'The Colonel goes, we will stay.' announced Shushkin, raising his voice against the wind and the high-pitched whine of the helicopter's turbine engines.

As the Sea King came into the hover, they saw a smoke marker being dropped to determine the wind direction. Their rescuer, clad in a bulky survival suit, was soon being winched down. Then he was among them: 'Does anyone speak English?'

'Take him,' said Shushkin, pointing at Koslov, 'He is badly injured.'

Belyakov pushed Koslov forward, then helped to attach the strop that would support his weight.

137

'We wait for a ship,' said Shushkin. 'Get him to a doctor.'

'We're not going to leave you lot out here!'

'Our ship is close,' insisted Shushkin. 'We wait!'

Koslov and the winchman rose up out of the sea. Aided by a crewman at the door, they were soon safely inside the helicopter. The winchman did not come down again. Instead he stood in the door and pointed to the north. He could see *Petrushka* ploughing through the waves towards them. Before the helicopter turned away, he dropped another smoke marker. Shushkin thanked him with a salute, which was returned.

As they tilted back and forth with the waves, it was difficult to see the ship for more than a few seconds at a time. When the helicopter turned back towards the coast, *Petrushka* was certainly a welcome sight. The wind was increasing, and the swells were getting higher. Even though rescue was surely only minutes away, Shushkin was not the only one who felt strangely uneasy. Their collective silence was broken by a muffled boom, followed by a rising column of white water as the explosion came to the surface. Fortunately they had drifted too far away for the concussion to have any effect.

Shushkin spoke for all of them. 'The torpedo!'

'A self-destruct device,' said Belyakov. 'Interesting.'

Petrushka hove to and lowered a rigid inflatable boat. It wasn't long before they were all aboard. Their comrades gave them dry clothes, hot chocolate and something to eat. They were all wondering the same thing: what would happen to their commander?

Chapter X

'What's so special about this torpedo?' asked Boxted.

'All I know at the moment is that it's called "Blue Diver". I'll have more for you when I get back from the Cabinet Office,' said Sir Stephen, picking up his briefcase. 'In the meantime, we'd better issue a D-notice. That should give the cabinet press secretary time to cobble together a statement. And call Neville Charlton, would you? He's the project manager at Spinney Heath. Mary has the number.'

It was going to be another late night at 140 Gower Street.

When he'd finished apologising, Charlton began to bring Boxted up to speed. 'The guard on duty was Jimmy Ruswarp. He's been with us for over twenty years. You couldn't meet a nicer bloke. During the war he drove a tank with the Desert Rats. He'd normally have been patrolling with Prince, a German Shepherd, but a few days ago the dog was struck by a car... one of his back legs got broken. He's on the mend now, though.'

'Frankly, I'm more interested in what actually happened. This is a secure line, so you can speak freely.'

'Sorry... yes... of course. From what we can gather whoever took it simply opened the crash gate to enter – and presumably leave – the airfield. There were some fresh tyre tracks left on the grass between the gate and the service road leading to the hangar, probably from a long wheel-base Land Rover. The padlock securing the hangar doors was picked. The torpedo was in its bespoke container, covered by a tarpaulin. It was replaced with a packing crate... the police say it was a professional job.'

'Any CCTV?'

'Still on the "to do" list, I'm afraid.'

'So, what you're telling me is that a top secret torpedo was protected by a dodgy padlock and some not exactly diligent patrols... by one man without his dog.'

'To be honest we never expected anything like this to happen. We only discovered it was missing when a US Navy P-3 came in for a systems integration test.'

139

'What's a P-3?'

'A maritime patrol aircraft, roughly comparable to our Nimrod.'

'How are the Americans involved?'

'Blue Diver's been their programme since our government decided to cancel it last year. The US Navy are going to retrofit the warhead on to their existing air-launched torpedoes. As we already have the know-how, duplicating the effort would have delayed things unnecessarily. They're very keen to have it deployed as soon as possible. This is all privileged information, of course. Classified.'

'I understand... thank you for your time.' *The Americans aren't going to be best pleased*, he thought. He was right.

Boxted ended his call to Charlton at 6.35pm. It was 1.35pm in Washington DC, and by then the Director of the CIA knew all about the shoot down. His source was a USAF RC-135 electronic intelligence (ELINT) aircraft that had been up from its Suffolk base for a routine 'collection' mission to the Baltic. When back over the North Sea, it had continued to monitor, classify and filter any transmissions that might be of interest – including those from the *Petrushka*. It was also listening-in on the UHF frequencies used by the RAF.

After receiving confirmation of the incident from their office at the US Embassy in Grosvenor Square, the CIA was able to brief the US Secretary of State. He then broke the news to the President, who was soon on the line to the PM. The leader of the Free World was assured that such a major incident would naturally be investigated with the utmost vigour. When the PM confirmed that a US exchange pilot had been flying the Phantom, the President didn't exactly rush to offer unequivocal support. Instead he wanted that little nugget – indeed any news of the entire incident – to be suppressed. 'Let's keep quiet about this,' he counselled, 'until we hear what Moscow has to say.' The PM concurred.

Barely an hour later, the COBR committee (named after the Cabinet Office Briefing Room at 10 Downing Street) was being chaired by the PM. Also present were the Foreign Secretary, the Home Secretary, the Secretary of State for Defence, the Chief of the Defence Staff, the First Sea Lord, Sir Stephen Sharp and 'C'.

The atmosphere was tense. There was no question of any further military response, but the displeasure of Her Majesty's Government 'should be made clear'. The PM also stressed the importance of 'restoring America's full confidence in the Special Relationship'.

'C' then effectively rained on the PM's parade by insisting that any leak concerning Blue Diver could only have come from the Americans. Sir Stephen agreed. MI5 had positively vetted everyone involved in the programme. The inner cabinet, and everyone else in the know about Blue Diver on the British side, were considered to be unimpeachable.

It was 10.30pm when Sir Stephen returned to his office – and he needed something stronger than sherry. He opened his drinks cabinet and brought out a cut glass decanter. 'There are times, Adrian,' he said, pouring a generous measure into each glass, 'when only the finest single malt will do.'

'Charlton was quite informative,' said Boxted, taking a sip. 'My report is on your desk.'

That report included an extract from MI5's latest security assessment, written just months earlier: 'The security measures in place at military airfields, including those involved in activities associated with R&D, are generally thought to be satisfactory. Military attaches and other diplomatic staff accredited to the Soviet Embassy and Embassies of other Warsaw Pact countries should be monitored in accordance with established procedures. Any suspicious activity should be communicated through the usual channels'.

Sir Stephen didn't take long to read it. 'Security at Spinney Heath was pretty lack-lustre, obviously.'

'Charlton did have a point when he said something like this would have been difficult to foresee. It was certainly audacious.'

'That's hardly going to placate our principal ally, is it? The PM wants to mend fences – which is going to be difficult given the degree of penetration involved. This operation was carefully planned – Moscow Centre must have an agent with top-level access, possibly in the Pentagon itself.'

'What about Lorenz? "C" certainly had his doubts about him, didn't he?'

141

'He's liaising with Langley as I speak. He should be able to tell us more over the next forty-eight hours.'

'Anything to add on Blue Diver?'

'Apparently it came... well, out of the blue. According to the First Sea Lord, some of our torpedo boffins put in some unpaid overtime.'

'So it's a bit like what happened at VW, when a small team of engineers came up with the Golf GTI...'

'Your analogy may be closer than you think, Adrian. It's original codename was JVX 229 – the reg number of the MGB driven by the head of the Underwater Warfare Research Establishment. Something of a tradition, apparently.'

'But not exactly secure...'

Inevitably, Saturday was a day of intense diplomatic activity. The Soviet Ambassador, Alexander Grebovkin, had been summoned to the palatial Foreign and Commonwealth Office in Whitehall by the Foreign Secretary, Nigel Greene. After Grebovkin was received, the two men were left quite alone and no notes were taken.

'Ambassador...thank you for coming. Do sit down.'

Greene was pinstriped, tall and fine featured, his hair shiny with Brylcreem. Grebovkin was shorter, square-shaped, with a stone face that could have been chiselled by the sharp winds off the Russian steppe. His manner was direct: 'You will please tell me the condition of the pilot.'

'Making good progress, according to the consultant I spoke to about an hour ago.'

'Then we expect him to be released into our care without delay.'

'It would be most unwise to move him in his present condition. He suffered a nasty gash to the forehead and lost a lot of blood. He also has a broken ankle. He's receiving the best possible care in one of our military hospitals, I can assure you of that.'

'Nevertheless I wish for one of our doctors to examine him. It is our right, as I think you know.'

'All in good time... you obviously know why you've been summoned here. Her Majesty's Government protests in the strongest possible terms about an action that was not only in flagrant breach of international law, but which also placed innocent lives at risk without any possible justification. May I remind you that one man – so far unidentified – was murdered on British soil. Such behaviour is completely unacceptable and cannot be tolerated. With immediate effect, we are suspending all commercial flights into the UK by any aircraft operated by the Soviet Union.'

'We reserve the right to respond in kind.'

'This is a very grave matter. I was hoping for something more constructive than a tit-for-tat response. An apology would be a welcome first step.'

'It was a civilian aircraft –'

'Carrying an illicit cargo. This is a matter of international law, of principle –'

'I am instructed to inform you that, at present, we are withholding any informations on the incident from press agencies. We do this in good faith, understanding that our pilot is to be returned... what is the word? Ah yes – discreetly, I think. As for the individual who was killed, we have no further use for him.'

Grebovkin's English wasn't perfect, but it was far better than Greene's Russian.

'Nevertheless,' said Greene, 'we intend to repatriate the body as soon as the formalities are completed.'

'As you wish. It may be of interest to know that I possess full transcript of the talk between your American pilot and his controller, recorded by the vessel which rescued our people.' He produced a single sheet of notepaper from his jacket, and took out his gold-rimmed reading glasses: 'This is what your pilot said: "The aircraft appears to civilian... no visible armament." I expect your RAF will have its own recording, should you require it.'

'I'm sure they have.'

'And, if you are going to suspend flights, I remind you that we did not retaliate despite many, many, aggressive overflights of our territory by your RAF and the American air forces. What would you have done if we had sent military aircrafts over your cities? Over Portsmouth or Birmingham?'

'That's all in the past. We haven't done anything like –'

'How can you justify such illegal activities?'

Greene was not going to be browbeaten. 'With great respect, you're hardly in a position to take the moral high ground – though I think we can both agree that not releasing any news of the incident at the present time would be in our mutual interest.'

'Then I think we have good basis for agreement. You know, both of us have seen war, when we fought together against the Fascist invader. You were in the navy, I think?' He said it with an expectant twinkle in his eye.

'Indeed. I was a gunnery officer in a destroyer escorting the arctic convoys to Archangel and Murmansk. I saw some fine ships and even finer men sent to the bottom. They helped to keep you in the war. I don't suppose that rates much of a mention in your version of history?'

'Those of us who were there do not forget your sacrifices. How strange that forty years ago we were comrades in arms? I was commissar in Murmansk. When it was over, I remember travelling thousands of kilometres... and seeing nothing but wasteland. Every hospital, every school, every village, every farm, every bridge, everything – all destroyed. And how many millions died? The price we paid is never appreciated in the West. Never again will we allow our Motherland to be threatened.'

'Our entire strategy is based on self-defence –'

'If only we could be so sure about the Americans...'

'They were once your Allies too, remember? You need to rebuild trust, not build more weapons.'

Chapter XI

In the three years he'd worked at the Pentagon, Rear Admiral Gene Bullett had never been so much as a minute late. After trying his home number several times with no reply, his secretary alerted the Defense Protective Service (DPS). They in turn asked the Washington State Patrol to check if the admiral's car had been involved in any sort of accident. It had not. A dispatcher was instructed to pull a cruiser off the interstate to make a house call.

At 10.37am two troopers rolled up outside a smart two-storey property in Stafford County, Virginia. The garage was slung underneath the living quarters. After trying the front door, one trooper went round the back while the other checked the garage door. It was a quiet neighbourhood – quiet enough to hear the low, steady beat of an idling V8 inside the garage.

They gained entry by breaking a pane in the back door. There was wire mesh glass in the access door to the garage. The light was on. They could see the admiral slumped in the driver's seat of his 1981 Pontiac Catalina Coupe. His head was tilted down and to the left. There was a hosepipe projecting through a small gap in the side window. The access and garage doors had been sealed with neatly-cut silver duct tape.

By noon special agents from the FBI were in the Pentagon, searching for answers. His secretary was understandably upset, and fought back tears as she mentioned a short-notice meeting called by the Chief of Naval Operations, the highest-ranking officer and professional head of the US Navy, that the admiral had been ordered to attend that morning 'without fail'.

News of his death would be withheld until his ex-wife and next of kin had been informed. That restriction did not apply to the CIA and certain other US intelligence agencies. After a conversation with the Director of the CIA at just after 6.30pm GMT, 'C' was in a position to brief Sir Stephen by telephone on this startling development in the Blue Diver affair.

'You remember the admiral I mentioned over lunch, Gene Bullett? He was found dead in his car this morning. It looks – or was made to look – like suicide. The car was in his garage at home, and so far everything points to carbon monoxide poisoning.'

'Did he leave a note?'

'Not unless you count Operation POWERPLAY – his plan for a first strike on the Soviet Union. The Director would only give me a brief outline before he left for the White House. It would seem that Blue Diver and POWERPLAY are inextricably linked. Now we know why he was so keen to rescue the programme... and why our friends in fur hats were determined to go to such extraordinary lengths to learn its secrets.'

'So that means Moscow Centre must have POWERPLAY... but how?'

'That's what the FBI is trying to find out. From what I can gather, Bullett was out on his own, a maverick. My prime source insists that no such plan was ever authorised – at least officially.'

'That's some consolation, I suppose. Did he seriously think his plan could ever work? If any tactical nukes survived – let alone any of the bigger stuff – we can assume the whole of Britain would be targeted. And if a general nuclear war broke out, vast populations from the East – not to mention what's left of the Red Army – might be forced to drive westwards in search of food and shelter. The terror and carnage doesn't bear thinking about.'

'We'd certainly have time to think about it, old chap, down in the T-site.'

(The 'T-site' or 'Turnstile' was a vast underground complex near Corsham in Wiltshire from where up to 4,000 government staff – including 'C' and Sir Stephen – would attempt to administer what was left of the country in the event of a nuclear war. The only families allowed would be of the Royal variety.)

'At least we'd still be alive...'

'Enjoying corn flakes and long-life milk for breakfast. After a couple of weeks any survivors would kill for that.'

Tuesday, 28th June, 10.00am GMT

Sophie had invited Gibson to a picnic on West Wittering Beach in Sussex. Before knocking on the door, he spotted her loading up the car. He waved, then strolled up to greet her. She was wearing cropped, wide leg pants in cream with a yellow tee shirt.

'You're in good time...'

'Well, it's quite a long drive down to the coast – would you like my bag?'

She placed it next to the picnic basket in the boot, which, like the VW Beetle's, is at the front. 'Believe it or not, Gerald's got another boot under the bonnet in the back, but it's right above the engine and I don't want the milk to curdle.'

'Perish the thought...'

'Shall we get going?'

'Ready when you are. You've certainly organised the weather – it's warming up nicely.'

The Fastback started first time, and she made excellent use of its 60 air-cooled horses, deftly shifting through the gears as they made there way on to Tower Bridge Road and round the Elephant and Castle.

'You seem to know where you're going,' he said.

'I studied the route last night – it's pretty straightforward, actually. There's a road atlas in the side pocket if we hit any jams.'

'Have you ever been unprepared for anything?'

'One of the first things we were told in the Corps is that prior preparation and planning prevents –'

'Piss poor performance.'

'Exactly – except we would never have said "piss".'

'Of course not... you were much too refined.'

'Refined might be pushing it a bit, though we scrubbed up rather well when the occasion demanded...'

After half an hour or so, they were on the A3, heading towards Guildford. He enjoyed sitting back and watching her at the wheel, the way she combined observation and anticipation with little or no hesitation. 'Is there anything you're not good at?'

'Don't ask me to dance. I move like Bambi – even when I'm sober.'

'I'd love to say that I was once the John Travolta of the lower sixth, but the truth is I'm just as bad – worse, probably.'

'What do you drive, Gary?'

147

'I decided to sell my old Mini Clubman years ago. All my cars come from the pool these days. I tend to prefer the Carlton, but there's quite a selection. The ones we use for surveillance have concealed two-way radios.'

'Including the odd council van?'

Gibson smiled. 'Or the gas board. We have our own little garage, tucked away in a quiet side street somewhere.'

'Somewhere...?'

'Strictly on a need-to-know basis.'

'I see... just because I didn't confide in you, I suppose?'

'It would've saved a lot of time...'

'It wasn't my decision, Gary. You of all people ought to know that.'

'Okay, okay – point taken. Let's just enjoy our trip to the seaside.'

She smiled. 'We can just be ourselves for a change.'

'It's getting a bit stuffy in here... mind if I use the air-con?'

'Go ahead – I think I will, too.'

They opened the quarterlights, adjusting the angle until the airflow was just right.

'One of my exes wanted me to fit a sunroof. That's one of the reasons why he's an ex. I didn't want to spoil the look of the car.'

'Even a factory-fitted one can leak, so why risk it?'

'My thoughts exactly.'

They took the A27 to Chichester, then followed the long, narrow road to the car park. The sea was sparkling under a cerulean sky. There was the balmiest of breezes. The sand looked pristine. It was already a perfect day.

'We'll have lunch while we wait for the tide to go out,' she said, unloading the car. She handed him the windbreak, rug and mallet, then picked up the picnic basket, Thermos flask and their sports bags. After a short stroll they picked a spot in front of the dunes and set everything up.

The sandwiches, wrapped up in greaseproof paper, were in plastic boxes. Another box contained chicken drumsticks wrapped in kitchen foil. A pack of cheese triangles and some cream crackers completed the menu. The milk was in a cup with a twist-off top.

148

'It hasn't curdled,' he said, taking a sniff.

She poured out the coffee, then offered him a salmon and cucumber sandwich.

'You've even cut the crusts off. Very posh.'

'This is a special occasion. I've also made some egg and tomato with salad cream…'

He eyed up the feast. 'I'll sink straight to the bottom if I eat all that lot.'

'We can always save some for later, Gary. You'll be hungry again after a swim.'

'We could've sailed over to Cowes for fish and chips if the old Shark had been seaworthy.'

'We can always come again. How's your sandwich?'

'Very tasty – I think I'll have another.'

'We're well protected here… the last thing we need is sand in our sandwiches.'

'And a few other places I'd rather not mention.'

Back at Gower Street, Sir Stephen was about to break for lunch with Boxted when Mary put through a call through from 'C' on his direct line.

'Is this going to spoil my appetite?' said Sir Stephen, pressing the speaker button. Boxted made a 50/50 hand gesture.

'My dear chap, would I ever do such a thing? First the good news – we're off the hook as far as that damned torpedo is concerned.'

'Really?'

'It seems that Bullett leaked it – from his own typewriter.'

'Do tell…'

'I must admit, the way they did it was most ingenious. When the Pentagon upgraded their "golf ball" electric typewriters, the admiral asked if he could buy the outgoing model, an IBM Selectric II. Permission was duly granted. When the FBI took it apart, they discovered some miniature magnetometers had been hidden in a support bar.'

'So every time he pressed a key…'

'Exactly – the selection of any character on the golf ball could be detected. The data was then compressed before being transmitted in bursts – probably to a vehicle parked nearby.'

149

'Which means Moscow Centre had POWERPLAY before anyone else.'

'There's only one other copy that we know about, and that was found in his safe. The State Department is now involved in a major damage limitation exercise. The pilot who flew the Phantom is being recalled to the States. I have it on good authority that decision was taken at the very top.'

'I have to ask the question: when did he acquire the typewriter?'

'Do you still suspect my brown eyed girl?'

'Was she in Washington at the time?'

'Purely coincidental, old chap, purely coincidental…'

'I don't like coincidences. And we only have her word for it that she rebuffed the approach from Moscow. That could easily have been a piece of theatre – a command performance.'

'Don't forget her deeds… among which is the small matter of saving Gibson's life.'

'I accept that she's undeniably impressive…'

'And ultimately she's my responsibility. I might as well tell you the FBI also found a swimming costume in his house, US size 4, bought from Bloomingdale's. It was gift wrapped…'

'More wind in his sails than you thought, perhaps? She happens to be a trained telegraphist for heaven's sake – that means she knows quite a lot about typewriters. QED.'

'Aren't you being rather hasty there, old chap? I happen to know that she wasn't the only one invited to his little soirée – Lorenz was there, too. There are now some long faces at Langley. Yesterday afternoon he took off from Miami on board a Colombian military flight to Bogota, ostensibly on a fact-finding mission. He's now in the Soviet Embassy there… shame we can't listen-in on the debriefing. At least we can now refocus on HENGIST – and leave Blue Diver to the Americans – they can hardly throw that back at us now. I'll let you know if anything else comes down the wires. As always, give my love to Felicity…'

Boxted had been listening intently. 'So you don't think Zoborski's in the clear?'

'No I don't, Adrian.'

'Perhaps I ought to mention that I agreed to release the Tokarev to her – she's going to register with a local gun club.'

That didn't seem to concern Sir Stephen. He stood up and walked over to the window. 'Is it thinking the unthinkable to suppose that Lorenz was sacrificed to protect her?'

'"C" has obviously discounted that possibility.'

'Let's hope he's right, Adrian – otherwise we might be dealing with the best penetration agent since Philby.'

West Wittering Beach, 2.51pm

The tide was now well on its way out. It was time for Sophie and Gibson to get changed.

'This isn't a nudist beach,' she said, 'so hold that towel around me. No peeping, if you don't mind. I'll do the same for you.'

As she stepped into her jet black swimsuit, she overbalanced slightly and had to lean against him.

'Now I know why you can't dance – no sense of balance.'

'It was only a lumpy bit of sand, that's all. You won't have any trouble with those big feet of yours.'

He didn't. He was soon in his two-tone blue swim shorts, and folded up his chinos and a polo shirt.

'You coming?'

'Not just yet. I think I'll just sunbathe for a bit. It might help to disguise these bruises.'

'The salt water won't do them any harm, you know.'

He took in that easy, graceful walk of hers, the arresting look back that made him feel like a king. He watched as she became a distant silhouette. Then she was in the water, swimming in one of the lagoons left by the ebbing tide. The sound of the sea caressing the beach began to make him feel sleepy. Soon he was dreaming of being on a tropical island, a Robinson Crusoe waiting for his Girl Friday. They would be equals, of course, always looking out for each other. He could see himself with her, collecting driftwood for fuel, paddling out through the surf in a skiff to go fishing...

She stayed out for 15 minutes, then came back. 'Earth calling Gary. Come in, Gary...'

'Sorry – I was miles away.'

'Come on, I'll race you to that sand bank.'

'I'm quite happy where I am.'

'We haven't come all this way for you to just sit here all day.'

She reached for his hand, and tried to pull him up. But he was stronger, and pulled her down on top of him. He kissed her, full on the lips. She didn't try to push him away. He could taste the sea. The contrast between the warmth of the sun and the coolness of her body felt delicious, electric.

'You're taking unfair advantage…'

'I don't care.'

He rolled her over, and kissed her again. 'I don't suppose I could stay over tonight?'

'Perhaps... on one condition: that you get off this beach and into the water.' She slid out from under him, picked up her hat and goggles, and started walking. She felt his hand on her waist as he caught up. 'You need to know that I like my independence, my own space. And we're bound to be apart for much of the time.'

'I can live with that. I owe you my life, but that's almost incidental. I'd still feel the same way about you if we'd just met out in the street somewhere. When I saw you in that police station, I think my heart literally jumped. I've never met anyone like you – but that doesn't mean I'm going to get under your feet like some dewy-eyed spaniel.'

'Just don't say you love me – not yet. I don't want you phoning me every day, either.'

'I'll send you a postcard.'

She smiled, then started to run. He managed to overtake her and was first into the water, but after that it was no contest. She was already stretched out on the sand bank as he found his footing and waded the last ten metres or so.

'What kept you?'

'My crawl is nowhere near as good as yours. Now, where were we?' He moved in for another kiss.

'Ah-ah-ah – I don't like being pawed in full public view, thank you very much. There are men out there with binoculars – and telephoto lenses for all we know.'

'They're probably just birdwatching – apart from the two blokes who pulled up in that red Cortina while you were busy under the bonnet – or was it the boot?'

'Our minders, I suppose?'

'Special Branch – we don't want anyone else taking a pop at us, do we?'

'Which reminds me – I'd like to put a few rounds through that Tokarev of mine.'

'Haven't you done enough of that for the time being? It's not as if you need the practice…'

'I'm not going to let what happened last week rule the rest of my life. They were bad men... they had it coming to them.'

'Okay – but the ammo's bound to be out-of-date for a start. And it will need to be inspected, cleaned and tested.'

'I've already seen to all that.'

'Really?'

'It was in remarkably good condition.'

'We should make a move soon,' he said, as a cloud shadow crept over them. 'Looks like there might be some weather coming in.'

They were not the only ones thinking of home. Major Rico Hamlee, his wife Suzy and Rico Jr, were halfway across the Atlantic in a Lockheed C-141 Starlifter jet transport, the same type of 'freedom bird' that, in the spring of 1973, had flown him back to the States from Tan Son Nhut air base in South Vietnam. Back in the hold was his Pontiac Firebird Trans Am, Rico Jr's new bicycle and – in addition to their luggage – some sticks of furniture they didn't want to leave behind. In the boot (he would call it the trunk) of the Firebird was his prized set of Jack Nicklaus golf clubs.

Tucked away in an envelope at the bottom of a suitcase was something that would not be shared during his scheduled interview with the Air Force Chief of Staff at the Pentagon. That something was a Polaroid of his Phantom with a red star stencilled on its left splitter-plate, one of the large moveable panels ahead of the jet intakes that automatically adjust the airflow into the engines. RAF technicians can be an irreverent lot, and SENGO (the senior engineering officer) had turned a blind eye while the 'kill' marking

153

was added. But it was oversprayed within minutes of the photos being taken – no one wanted to risk a court-martial.

Another Polaroid had gone to Pilot Officer Brian Hopkins, who would shortly be on his way to join a Phantom detachment on the Falkland Islands. He did not exactly greet the news of this politically motivated posting with unrestrained enthusiasm. Hopkins' mood changed considerably when his station commander went on to explain that in return for six months in the South Atlantic, he would be sent for 15 hours grading on the Chipmunk, the pretty pilot trainer he remembered from his days with the Air Cadets. If he passed, the long process of training to become a fighter pilot would begin.

XV547 had, meanwhile, been flown out to a deep maintenance unit for a complete overhaul and repaint. Never again would it be coded 'B' for Bravo. It would subsequently be allocated to a different squadron entirely. This decision was not related to what happened when they returned from the mission. Perhaps sensing they had little to lose, Hamlee had decided to beat-up the airfield in comprehensive fashion. The circuit was clear, and with fuel to spare he announced their arrival with a high speed run at Mach 0.9, followed by a rocket-like zoom climb in full afterburner.

By the time they landed, the noise complaints were coming in from the usual suspects. There were, however, far more calls asking for a repeat performance!

And what of Koslov? 'Discreet' was indeed the word to describe his departure from Heathrow earlier that afternoon in a specially chartered air ambulance – a Swiss-registered Lear Jet. He was met at Geneva Airport by General Kubishev, who assured him that the mission had been far from a failure. Furthermore Koslov was now a Hero of the Soviet Union, awarded for his 'valorous conduct in Afghanistan and elsewhere'.

Before it arrived at Cullingthorpe, detailed photographs had been taken of Blue Diver's all-important electronics. While its technological secrets were being unpicked, Soviet submarines would be handled more evasively. Future designs were expected to be quieter and deeper diving.

At West Wittering, Sophie and Gibson had returned to the Fastback. She produced an old washing up liquid bottle full of water and a hand towel, and handed them over to him.

'You go first – it's to get the sand off your feet.'

'So it's not to clean the windscreen?'

'You can do that as well, but I've got a chamois for that.'

When they were ready to depart, he was about to open the passenger door when she threw him the keys.

'You can drive. The clutch bites fairly high, just so you know.'

Despite the advice, the first few changes were somewhat clunky. 'I think I'm beginning to get the hang of it... I've never driven one of these before.'

'Not even a Beetle?'

'Can't say I have – virtually all the pool cars are British.'

'You're doing alright now.'

'I'm enjoying myself, actually. In fact, I can't remember the last time I enjoyed myself half as much as I have today.' He glanced across at her, smiling. She was smiling, too.

'By the way, I saw your friend Adrian yesterday.'

'I thought we'd agreed –'

'We're on our way home now, so I don't see why I shouldn't mention it.'

'What did he have to say?'

'I think he just wanted to clear the air. I asked him why he'd chosen you to look after me.'

'They were desperate.'

She laughed. 'That's what he said.'

'We're stretched pretty thin at times – and this happens to be one of them.'

'Actually, Adrian spoke very highly of you.'

'He's a good scout, no doubt about that.'

'He helped you through your bad patch, didn't he?'

'How much did he tell you?'

'He didn't say anything – he said he'd leave it up to you.'

'You might as well know – you're going to find out anyway. It happened in Northern Ireland. There weren't all that many of us over there – our role was purely supportive. We managed to get a line on one of the IRA's top bomb makers. The intel was that he was coming up from South Armagh, and that meant he either already had a device or that he was coming to assemble one. He knew all about counter-surveillance, so we had to be on our toes. Our informer gave us a name and we had a good description. I happened to be at one of the checkpoints in West Belfast when he came through in an old Ford Anglia – it wasn't on our list. He was driving, and there was a heavily pregnant woman next to him. She said she was having contractions, and that he was taking her to hospital. So the soldiers hurried up the checks and waved them through.

'He'd used the wife and car of a man being held hostage, someone entirely innocent – not a known sympathiser. By the time we realised what had happened, he'd swapped cars and got clean away. A few days later a bomb disposal expert was killed walking up to a Bedford van on the Falls Road. The device was detonated remotely – cold-blooded murder. If only I'd been a bit more observant...'

'You can only do so much, Gary.'

'The man who took that long walk, Simon Drinkwater, had only presented to us the week before. He was a good bloke with a wicked sense of humour. Not just gallows humour, either – though there's plenty of that in the bomb disposal business. He talked us through the latest devices, including the type that killed him.

'I suppose I hit the bottle pretty hard. It was only for a few days, mind – I didn't see any dark woods or anything like that. I soon pulled myself together, but not quickly enough for my dear old section leader. He reported me for being drunk on duty. That's when Boxted stuck up for me. Without him I'd have been out on my ear.'

'You would have been difficult to replace. I suppose if he hadn't intervened, we'd never have met, would we?'

'I did say to him that you were the best assignment I'd ever had. I'm not sure I believe in fate, though – I'm just glad you came along when you did. And I'm not just speaking professionally.'

It was another two-hour drive back to Bermondsey, yet the journey seemed to take half the time.

156

They unloaded the car against the backdrop of a beautiful sunset. She turned the key in the lock and led him into the living room. 'Just dump everything here for the time being. I'll sort it out later.'

'Mind if I take a shower?'

'Of course not – you'll find a clean towel in the airing cupboard.'

'Care to join me?'

'There's not enough room in there.'

'I meant in the shower…'

'Is there a drought or something? You just go ahead.'

He was about to turn on the shower when he heard the phone ring. It was 9.21pm. He listened as she picked up.

'Oh hello, Adrian. 'I wasn't expecting –'

'I've some very bad news for you.'

'It's about Dad, isn't it?'

'I'm afraid so…'

Gibson could tell by her tone of voice that all was not well. He dressed quickly and walked back into the living room.

'How did it happen?'

'We think he was poisoned by the milk or orange juice delivered to his doorstep this morning. It seems he realised something was wrong almost immediately. He was found by the front gate…'

'Thank you for letting me know.'

'Is Gary with you?'

'We've just had the most brilliant day. And now this… it's always been at the back of my mind that he wasn't really safe, that someone would want to close his file. Now they have.'

'I'm sorry, but you'll be expected to make the formal identification. If you need any help with the funeral arrangements…'

'You're very kind. Now, if you don't mind, I'd like a little time to myself.'

'Of course, Sophie. But you're also in danger. Can you put Gary on, please?' She beckoned him over.

'How much did you hear?'

'Enough.'

'She'll have to go to a safe house – until we can organise something more permanent.'

157

She was close enough to hear what was being said. 'I'm not going anywhere tonight.'

'Did you get that?' asked Gibson.

'I'm hardly going to argue, not at a time like this.'

Gibson put down the phone. He turned towards her. She came forward. They hugged each other. He could feel her tears. It was a singular moment, the most moving he had ever experienced. The need to kiss her was almost overwhelming. By the time they moved apart, her tears had subsided. Her eyes were now full of intense, burning anger. 'They never give up. Never. Well, neither will I.'

'Look, I know how you must feel...'

'No you don't – no one can. I'll find out who did this stupid, senseless thing. And when I do, I'm going to do more than just even up the score.'

'You don't work for an assassination bureau.'

'Then I'll resign, go freelance.'

'You won't stand a chance, Sophie, not on your own.'

'We'll see about that...'

THE END

Sophie will return in CODENAME CAPELLA